HOW TO TRAIN YOUR WITCH

BETTINA M JOHNSON

AQUA RAVEN PUBLISHING

How to Train Your Witch

ISBN: 978-1-7350692-2-7 (paperback)

Cover Art by StunningBookCovers.com

CHAPTER 1

*D*id you ever dream of skipping school? Maybe you were one of those brave rebels who did and managed to get away with it. Not me. I'm too goody-goody. I had obedience and propriety ingrained in me by my mother and broke out in hives if I jaywalked. Not that I wasn't trying very hard as of late to break the shackles of my upbringing and live a little. I'd ripped those 'Do Not Remove' tags off my pillow just last week.

I know, shocking!

I am not complaining. I comprehend that I have to learn my craft because, untrained, I am a walking hazard at best—utter mayhem at my worst. Let's just say mayhem has been my middle name as of late and call it a day. Too much reckless magic and inadvertent spell faux pas have been my calling card, and I want that to change. Hopefully, the townsfolk will stop having adverse reactions every time they see me pass.

Oh—spells—magic? Yes. You see, my name is Lily Sweet, and I am a witch.

No, I am not in a twelve-step program for the delusional.

I am a bona fide, card-carrying witch from a long and vener-able line of witches—many of them dark. This does not mean I am malicious or have relatives in tune with their Wicked Witch of the West side. However, the jury is still out on my great-grandmother, Adriana. And I have a cat named Wicked; both are equally capable of being one hundred percent pure, unadulterated evil.

And that's on a good day.

I discovered I was a witch not too long after arriving in Sweet Briar, Georgia, my hometown. I never knew it was my hometown because my mother fled this part of the country and moved me way up to the Catskill mountains of New York State. She assumed badass witches were after me. She was correct, but not in the way she believed. And had Jessica Croy Sweet just stayed and sought the help of family, well, things might have been different where I was concerned as far as my knowledge of all things witch. I didn't return until after her death and cryptic instructions she'd left behind, suggesting I cautiously go seek out my Georgia roots. Being clueless left me at quite a disadvantage.

You see, most young witches are in command of their abilities by the time they are thirteen or fourteen. Here I am, twenty-five, and because of my upbringing, I have just finished my first whole week of witch school. I was supposed to start on December 1st. However, due to my freaking out about my days being micromanaged and grumbled complaints to my great granny, she forced me to start early. Even though I was technically still recuperating from yet another attack on my person.

Her ire is one reason I am in classes half the day, five days a week.

The person who attacked me this time around was, well, me! I slapped my hand to my forehead after an errant spell went awry, knocking my friend Lorcan out cold in the process. I blinded myself for twenty-four hours or so, and the result was a lengthy hospital stay. OK, so I was also trying to disarm a tilty-head, creepy, and possibly possessed teenager, and my cousin Nora, who hates me, but that's another story altogether. I was in the hospital for over a week. It is now December 5th, and I'm in the second whole week of lessons. I can say, with absolute certainty, I will not survive until Christmas. It's been nice, but I'm about to perish at the hands of two randy cougars, a tiny replica of Reba McEntire, and a demon-spawn from hell.

That demon-spawn is—you guessed it—Adriana Dolce, my great-grandmother on my father's side.

If the witch Council in our town ever manages to find my errant dad, Charles, I have a bone to pick with him about running off and leaving me to fend for myself with all these crazy relatives of mine. My father's side and my mom's. The Dolce clan is all Italian, very powerful, and pretty much runs our small corner of the world. The Croy side, my mother's people, are Scottish and equally esteemed, but less in your face about it—and not as in charge around here as the Dolce's. I'm a Sweet because my grandfather decided to change the Italian surname to its American counterpart.

Are you as confused as I am? Sorry about that. But I digress.

All you need to know is I am a prisoner. A hapless student, thrust in a classroom where free-thinking and coloring outside the lines will get me, not a firm rap on the knuckles, oh no. That would be too kind. I get exploding potions and evaporating eyebrows. Seriously. I managed to burn one down to stubble and decided to tell everyone it was a fashion statement.

"Liliana! Stop daydreaming and tell me why you need to center yourself, clear your thoughts, and then release your spell?"

That would be the demon-spawn, uh, Adriana. It's time I focus on today's lesson before she gives me detention.

"Because if I don't, there is a good chance a stray thought can shape the spell, causing it to not only misfire but take on different properties than what I intended?"

"Brava. And what is a good way to clear your mind and center yourself?" Adriana demanded.

"Yoga?" I knew I was asking for it with that snarky comment when my granny scowled at me and crossed her arms, tapping her foot for good measure.

I shrugged and sheepishly managed a slight grimace of a smile before mumbling out my answer, "I focus on an internal flame, making my mind see it even though it isn't there. Then I bring it up and out of me in the form of whatever spell I am casting. And I need to accomplish this task, efficiently and quickly, especially if and when I find myself in battle." After giving my answer, I observed Adriana's face go from sullen to mild satisfaction and knew I'd nailed it.

Hallelujah.

Now to be able to *do* it.

"Liliana, cara. Come and sit a minute and listen to me." Adriana addressed me in a moment of sympathetic understanding. Unusual for her, which left me momentarily stunned, so I listened raptly to whatever it was she was about to impart.

"Liliana. I know you are upset at having to be back in school at your age. I know you aren't lazy or whining just to hear yourself. Heaven knows you had a very rigid and unusual upbringing in light of Jessica's neurosis, and I understand that you have a lot of socializing—among other things —to catch up on."

Adriana patted my knee and continued, "I am very proud of how hard you are working getting the studio up and running. I know you plan on tackling much of the renovations to your home as soon as you are making a profit, but you cannot neglect your witch studies. Ever. Not anymore. Especially after seeing what your talents were when your file arrived from the Council." Adriana stated emphatically, "you are a powerful witch."

"Grandmother, don't take this as me whining, please. But how am I supposed to glean how serious all this witchy education is if you won't let me see my talents?" I cried. I'd asked for one week now to find out what I could do magically, but every time I did, my great-grandmother had one excuse after another as to why she wanted to wait to share my specialties, and it had my nose out of joint. I already knew I was an anomaly, especially when you considered most witches had two, maybe three, abilities at most. I had seventeen.

Yeah. I'm impressed myself.

Every witch can do elemental magic, like move a glass or open a window with minimal effort. But unique abilities manifest at an early age, usually at puberty, and each witch had their talents recorded in the Witch Council. My cousin Andrea was adept at cloaking. She could make herself, or others, invisible and was able to eavesdrop with abandon. Her secondary talent was the ability to muddle sound, so people had a difficult time making out what she was saying in a private conversation.

Lorcan, my friend, and landlord of sorts—he was letting me rent a spot he owned directly next door to his mechanic shop—was an empath and walking hot water bottle. I kid you not. He could make you feel calm, safe, and warm just by a touch, or better yet, a big bear hug. He uses his talents in the children's ward at our local hospital when volunteering, making anxious parents feel inner calm and bringing the little patients' nerves down to a comforting level, making him one popular witch. Everyone loved Lorcan in our town!

My one-time boyfriend and a detective not to be trifled with, Brian Chase, was a Veritum. They were seekers of truth of the highest order, and one breath of yours across his olfactory senses could make or break you if you were guilty of some transgression. Brian would know in an instant if you were lying or being truthful. A useful, albeit scary, talent. I say, one-time boyfriend because we are on the outs after I decided his moving way too fast, and being a tad on the authoritarian side wasn't the type of man I thought I needed to be with at the moment. If ever. I was rather proud of myself for maturing over these last few weeks, knowing my experience with men had been sketchy at best. I knew I needed to trust my instincts more.

My great-grandmother, Adriana, had quite a list of talents. She could turn people into animals or vice-versa, or so I was told. She could animate objects and bend people's wills, especially since she could read minds with ease. Rumor had it she could also bind souls and lock them away in jars, although I doubted the validity of that one. I knew she could bind people and even ghosts. I saw her whisk one Edith Plank, an unfortunate librarian who wound up getting murdered and returning as a ghost, up against a wall and held her there against her will for a time. Rather impressive and helpful if one found oneself needing to coral ghosts, something I hoped I wouldn't need to enact much in my future. Thankfully, Edith has since moved on. Adriana could also hurl nasty spells that would go boom at anyone in her path and do so with a quirky smile on her face. Few folks around here wanted to get on her wrong side.

I was one of the only people not to fear my diminutive imp of a granny, and it usually got me in more trouble than it was worth. I knew she was one-hundred-percent correct and that I needed to become a proficient witch in a hurry. I didn't understand why I had to do it on her terms and without full knowledge of my talents. I wasn't petulant. I had a right to know! What if I inadvertently let some perilous and nasty poof of power out of my fingertips and blasted an unsuspecting victim to smithereens? If I knew what to expect, I could be cautious and careful at all times.

"What if withholding knowledge from me causes me to whack some poor unfortunate with my power? It would be best if you let me know what I'm capable of achieving. It will be on your head if I do someone harm." I tried once again to coerce granny with reason.

"Pulease! Right now, you are barely able to keep ice cream on a popsicle stick. The last thing we need is you over-thinking everything because you get a gander at your long list of suspected abilities. Suspected, mind you. I haven't verified anything as of yet. That will come once you master the basics of witchcraft and spell casting. Until then, kiddo, you are staying under the blindfold I've put on you." Adriana sniffed.

"Fine. Be that way. Don't blame me if you forget to duck." I waved my hand in her direction and watched in horror as an errant bolt shot out of my fingertips and zinged straight into Adriana's hair, causing it to explode in electric static amazingness. It loosened the tight bun she wore, causing her hair to stand straight out from her scalp like a spiky glowing halo.

I guess I forgot to focus on that inner flame, huh?

* * *

"Did she really have you stay an extra hour?" My cousin Andrea was nothing if not supportive of me and was one of the best things about being thrust into a vast family such as mine.

"Yes. And I don't want to talk about it. Because now I have

additional homework as well. Stupid, dumb, big, fat, mouth. Idiotic disobedient fingers." I grumbled.

"How do you feel about the rest of the lessons? Are Hermione and Hortense as rigid as Grandmother? Tanaquil is formidable but fair. I had her myself when I was in school." Andrea's voice trailed off as I lobbed a glare in her direction.

"Yes, Dre. But the last time you were in school was just about the last time I was. I am afraid Adriana will insist I enroll in Sweet Briar Elementary before all is said and done! They'll shove me into one of those horrid little desks, and all the kids will laugh at me behind my back! I will look like Buddy in Elf and be the town laughingstock, oversized and clueless."

Andrea sniggered but gave my arm a sympathetic pat before flopping back on my bed, pulling Wicked, my obstinate feline, on top of her.

"You can't let Granny get to you, Lily. The two of you are so alike—that's why you butt heads so frequently." Andrea began scratching Wicked under her chin, and the purring commenced in earnest.

"Bite your tongue. I am nothing like that woman. I still can't believe you tried to make me believe Grandfather Antonio is as sinister as she is. There is no way that sweet old man is anything like Adriana. Grandfather is a darling little gnome who likes to garden and feeds birds and butterflies. Heck, he doesn't even chase the squirrels away from his feeders. He's a big softy." I reached out to pet Wicked, but she swiped at my hand and hissed. I eyed Jake's old baseball bat hanging above my bedroom door and gave her a pointed looked. She yawned in response.

"That softy cursed his old nemesis, Doc Warren, now since retired, but at the time the town pharmacist, without telling anyone about it. The older men in town played bocce on the village green before moving the courts to the park.

Doc Warren was instrumental in this move because he'd continuously complain about wayward bocce balls flying at the giant glass window at the pharmacy.

"The year of the final tournament on the village green is when the incident happened. About one week later, his wife finally got around to informing us he never came home from the bocce tournament. We figured out grandfather turned him into a sheep! We had wondered why one showed up near the drugstore. The poor thing was bleating and trying to get in the automatic doors, but the manager kept chasing him out. That his wife didn't mind her spouse went missing, especially because he tended to sing at the top of his lungs while sleepwalking, made us all realize she probably enjoyed the respite."

"Please. There is no way I can even begin to believe such a tale," I stated, convinced Andrea was trying to pull a fast one. He was all of four-foot-eleven and total marshmallow fluff. There wasn't the slightest chance he'd be such a mean-spirited rascal. Unless I witnessed him performing malicious machinations of magic upon another, I steadfastly refused to believe him possible of such deeds. I continued my observation, "Grandpa is a cream puff."

"OK, cuz. Believe what you will. But that man can give old Beelzebub a few lessons in mischief. He's been in a mood lately. It might be because he has a new nurse, but I think he is upset we haven't had a massive family get-together, especially around the holidays. Oh! Not that it is your fault. He doesn't blame you since, um."

Yeah, since for Halloween and Thanksgiving, I had managed to wind up in the emergency room. I get it. I am turning into the holiday jinx in my family. Hopefully, no evil asshats will show up in the next few weeks and have me destroy Christmas as well.

Sigh. I'm actually in a heightened state of anxiety, just

thinking about mistletoe, cookies, wreaths, lights, and trees. I don't want to be a downer, though. After the last incident, where I almost got bested by whatever the heck it was that possessed Rowan Nightingale, I have resolved myself to enjoy life. I need to embrace my family and friends, hugs and holidays quickly, and being an extrovert even if the thought makes me want to find a cave and hide in it.

New year, new me, and all that.

I contemplated young Rowan. She had just turned nineteen and worked for June Carter, my mom's one-time best friend and the woman I am renting my apartment from while I decided what to do with the home I inherited. Talk about an introvert. Rowan makes me seem like a regular party girl, a cheerleader-type, which I am most definitely not. I know the Council still has her in their care, in some type of psychiatric ward attached to our local hospital. The witch clerics have been trying to figure out what possessed her, making her murder our town's librarian, Edith Plank. No one is sure if someone influenced her thoughts. She seems an easy target for some nefarious sorcery. Or if she acted alone and is an insane teen who was bent on getting the boy she liked at all costs. Either way, she has creeped me out to epic proportions, and I wondered if I will ever look at her in the same light if the Elders deem her a victim in all that came to pass.

That I was a victim, even if the reason I became injured had to do with my inability to control my magic rather than a direct attack by Rowan, was a given. Rowan, or whoever was pulling her strings as puppet master. I am still sore over the fact I managed to knock myself out. I am embarrassed that I shot a few errant bolts into Lorcan. But more than anything since the incident, I had a permanent sour disposition every time my thoughts turned to my cousin Nora and the fact she escaped and still has not been found, despite the police having searched far and wide for her.

What had me out of sorts was that our newest deputy, Gordon Delaney, managed to sweet-talk the sheriff into dropping all charges that were brewing concerning my deplorable cousin. They had the all-points bulletin on her called off. I hated to admit it to myself, but other than pulling a gun on Lorcan, which sounds terrible until someone informed us it was a prop gun and not the real thing, she hadn't done anything to warrant a police arrest. Her past indiscretions at college notwithstanding. All Nora demanded was the box I carried in my hand that I managed to find, with the help of a mysterious water sprite or magical creature that lived in Nichols Pond. I didn't hand it over to my cousin.

Yeah. I know—weirdness all around me, twenty-four, seven.

The box contained a ring left to me by my Aunt Adelaide, if I'm to believe the voice that magically began to speak after I opened it. There were times, especially in the wee hours of the morning, where I was afraid that I'd lost my mind. I began doubting all that had happened to me since leaving New York State and moving here to Sweet Briar. Then I'd gaze down at the beautiful ring that I never removed from my right hand, in the shape of a sweet briar rose, our town's namesake, and I could feel the power radiating from it and knew I wasn't a nut case. Much.

"I don't even want to think about Christmas. I haven't done a bit of shopping and don't know what to buy for anyone." I whined as Andrea gave me a keen look.

"You, dear cousin, are worried about where you will wind up and which relatives' nose will get out of joint if you aren't celebrating in their home. This fretting doesn't have anything to do with gift buying. You know we are all easy-going and keep it simple and cheap but heartfelt. A candle, homemade cookies, a simple token of your affection. You are using this as an excuse because you don't want to hurt anyone's feelings." Andrea sat up, shifting Wicked to her lap.

"Great-grandpa is upset for that very reason. Stevie Junior was talking about going on a ski trip for the long Christmas weekend, and my mom was making noises that she thought it a grand idea, and we'd all go and drag you with us—effectively taking you away from the rest of your relatives. Your Aunt Iona heard about it when Cousin Sophia mention it to my dad at the café. Iona had a meltdown. Stevie quickly nixed his plans, and a tentative peace resumed. That said, it's not your fault. You have nothing to do with any of this. Other than you are loved so much, everyone wants you with them for the holidays. I get that it's stressful, and you feel guilty."

She wasn't wrong with that proclamation. I had the same problem for Thanksgiving, except the untimely attack meant I spent that holiday laid out and dodged a bullet, even though it wasn't an enjoyable escape. This time around, I knew I'd have to decide which one of my aunts I'd spend Christmas Day with, and I had a feeling, no matter how I tried to appease them, I'd have hurt feeling and stress galore. Especially in light of this news. I groaned and flopped back onto the pillows on my loveseat.

"Hey, look on the bright side," Andrea exclaimed, "perhaps some other calamity will hit, and you'll knock yourself out cold again!"

I tossed a pillow at her head; only it bonked into Wicked, who ran, protesting loudly, from the room. Uh oh. I'd be paying for that little mistake later.

CHAPTER 2

"*W*ell, I didn't leave it there, so it must have been you who did." The voice that resonated around the shop was shrill and set my frayed nerves on edge.

"You know I don't play games. This silliness has you written all over it," was the reply.

I wasn't quite awake the next day and had my head down on the counter at A Tale of Two Witches Tea Shoppe. The Winters sister's new loose tea and tisane shop, where it was more potions and less brew than the average tourist should feel comfortable with, but for some reason, the business was thriving. I wasn't sure if it was because the duo were savvy businesswomen or their over-the-top witchy schtick went over well with the tourists who embraced our town's folksy magic vibe; maybe it was a bit of both. The ladies were going back and forth over some mysterious note they'd found tacked to their front door and were blaming each other for having left it for the other to discover. I couldn't figure out what the big deal was until one of the ladies, Hortense, I think, shoved it in my face.

"What do you make of this, Lily?" I glanced up, and it

was, indeed, Hortense who thrust said note under my nose. I blinked, bleary-eyed and angry, then blanched. The message on the piece of paper looked like one of those weird ransom notes you saw in the movies, complete with tiny letters cut out of newspapers, magazines, and other forms of advertising. It was creepy, but the words seemed harmless:

TO MAKE CHRISTMAS FUN, BRING ITEMS FOR TREE, SOMETHING TO EAT, ENOUGH TIMES THREE, GET THIS DONE, NO TIME TO WASTE, THE BIG DAY IS COMING, SO HURRY, POST-HASTE!
(Village square – Christmas Eve – be there, or else!)

"WHAT ON EARTH?" I peered at the sisters, who gave me matching looks of utter joy. It was disconcerting as they were beaming at me in a somewhat maniacal way.

"Don't you see? It's a riddle of some sort! I wonder what it means?" Hermione, the more reticent of the two, although grinning along with Hortense, had all the tell-tale signs of worry showing, as her forehead was creased, and she was wringing her hands. "You don't think we should take it seriously, do you? I mean, on the surface, it appears harmless. But the 'or else' could mean someone is unstable or joking, or..."

"Or they want us to show up with food and gifts and think we have nothing better to do on Christmas Eve since we're new in town...it must be a secret admirer. That means men. Eligible men! It must be a blind date!" Hortense seemed pleased with herself, and after much deliberation, Hermione did as well.

Wait a minute. There was no mention of gifts, and there

was no way a couple of men could possibly get through the amount of requested food. Could they?

"I'm not sure..."

"But of course, it must be two suitors! Sister, dear, I'm sorry I accused you of leaving this note on the door! It looks like we have dates for Christmas Eve!" Hortense clapped her hands and did a little sashay-wiggle-dance in place.

"Yes, but..."

"Oh! Whatever shall we wear, Tee-Tee? I think this calls for new outfits, don't you?" Hermione clapped her hands together and brought them up under her chin. Her eyes were sparkling like diamonds as she continued, "We simply cannot be caught dead in those old rags we have hanging in our closets, nasty old frocks... let's go shopping tomorrow, post-haste! Get it? Like the note said....' post-haste!' This is so exciting!" Giggling like an ingénue and not the forty-some-thing middle-aged woman she was, Hermione ran around the shop, setting tables for the morning rush. Then again, what did I know? With how long witches lived in my world, maybe the two sisters were still considered ingénues in some circles. Just not my circles.

Oh, who was I kidding? The two Winters sisters appeared to be in their early forties and were knockouts in an over-the-top; they could be strippers, or Vegas showgirls, in sequins and trailing feathered boa's kind of way.

Both wore way too much makeup and favored fake eyelashes and henna hair dyes; Hortense the purple eggplant color and Hermione a wine burgundy one. Their hair was big, like eighties Aqua Net hairspray big, and it matched their ebullient personalities. They might not be everyone's cup of tea, no pun intended considering their profession, but they indeed turned heads. They must have had some power over the opposite sex--they were both on the hunt for husbands' number four. I wasn't quite sure of what happened to

Misters' one, two, and three. I didn't know the ladies well enough yet to get that personal by making such queries.

Rumor had it they offed at least one of their spouses, each. Still, I didn't particularly appreciate listening to nasty gossip, considering the sources seemed to be disgruntled wives whose husbands had wandering eyes when the duo chose to strut by. Yes, they often strutted, and one couldn't blame the men because it wasn't just husbands who stared; everyone did. They had that effect on the town.

I had potions lessons with them every day, Monday through Friday, at six in the morning. At first, Adriana had scheduled my time at seven, but the sisters opened their doors for business at that hour, relegating me to the earlier time slot. I did my best to learn as they flew around the shop, preparing for the day and their plentiful customers.

The tea shop seemed like nothing any tea shop anywhere else would ever think to be—potion bottles in every shape, color, and size lined shelves and had catchy names like, 'Tisane of Bad Blood Begone,' or 'Elixir of Love's Lost Returning.' They brewed distinctive loose-leaf teas from the world over and added herbs grown and dried by Samantha Fairburn over at Fox Den Herbals. Customers would come in for tea and scones, get a sympathetic ear from Hermione or Hortense and walk out with a tonic to add to their loose tea purchase that would soothe all nerves or bring money or love, success, or a cure. Whether or not these potions worked was up in the air, but it didn't seem to stop people from flocking to the quirky shop and enjoying the entertaining duo.

"Ladies, I don't think..."

"Oh! Lily, dear, we almost forgot you were still here! What with this mystery note? Yes, now, where were we? Ah, yes. What is the best herb to infuse to make a soothing tisane that elevates the mood but doesn't bring anxiety or nervous energy along with its pleasant, uplifting properties?"

Well, OK, then. If the sisters didn't want to hear my opinion on the matter, I could move on.

"Borage?" I replied, hoping I remembered correctly and knew I had when Hermione glowed at me, nodding in the affirmative.

"Such a wonderful herb. I prefer it cooled once brewed and made into an iced tea. It has such a wonderful cucumber taste, perfect on a summer day!"

Hortense came back over to where I was sitting and placed a small purple glass vial with a matching stopper in front of me and gave me a list of ingredients on a piece of paper.

"Now, for a more ominous potion this weekend, I want you to gather these items on the list and follow the instructions I have written down. Follow them exactly, my dear, even if they sound off. I'd like to see how you do when concocting a potion that can negatively affect someone since your magic falls in the dark spectrum. No, no worries. This won't harm anyone per se, but, well, give it a go and let's see what you come up with on Monday, OK?" I eyed the list dubiously but agreed, then hopped down off my stool and gladly accepted a to-go cup of Earl Grey with a little something added that I suspected would make me less glum. Hermione winked as she handed it to me, and who was I to argue? I've been a grumpy, morose curmudgeon ever since my lessons started in earnest, especially when I would be making a potion called 'Leave Them in the Dust.' Whatever that meant!

* * *

"UGH. KILL ME NOW." Despite whatever pick-me-up Hermione added to my tea, I was still dragging a couple of hours later as Lorcan stood over my prone form, commiserating with my woeful and pathetic grousing by patting my shoulder. As I had my face buried in the cushion of the sofa I was lying on, I couldn't see the smile on his face, but I could hear it in his voice as he told me he'd prefer it if I remained alive.

"Easy for you to say. You can wake up at a normal hour, have breakfast, then head to work," I mumbled, the toss pillow I had over my head muting my kvetching. "I get up before the sun. I startle the birds in nearby trees, even. And do you know what those two sisters give me every morning upon my arrival?"

"Tea?" Lorcan replied, and I could tell he was holding back laughter at this point.

"Tea! They give me tea!" I shouted, turning on my side to glare up at my friend, who was now openly fighting his amusement at my acerbic demeanor.

"Who the heck drinks tea at that ungodly hour? I need java. Leaded. The real deal, not some decaffeinated, washed-down junk. How am I expected to function, let alone tackle making proper potions if I am sleep deprived and lethargic?" I threw the pillow across the room and sat up, groaning as my back protested from all the heavy lifting I had been doing around my studio.

"The British?" Lorcan suggested as I gave him a sour look that must have been a winner because he barked out a laugh then sat down next to me, pulling me into a friendly one-armed hug.

"Hardy har-har. You are a riot. I don't care if the British want tea first thing in the morning. Let them have all the tea they want. I'm American. I need my coffee!"

Just then, Andrea came rushing up the steps, joining us in

my makeshift office. I used the loft area as an office and loved standing at the railings gazing down at my work area below. The sunlight came streaming in from above, diffused by the ornate colored glass via a stellar round skylight. We'd uncovered it recently after decades of being hidden by a local Kudzu vine, notorious for swallowing anything and everything in its path.

"Have you seen this? I found it on dad's café door this morning when I went to open it up." Andrea held out a note, and I was shocked to see a replica of the one the Winters sisters had tacked to their door. I was going to mention this curiosity when Lorcan piped up that he, too, found one just like it, but on the windshield of his truck, tucked under the wiper blade.

"Seriously?" I asked, peering at both my friends in alarm. "Hermione and Hortense received one as well. What the heck is going on? What do you think it means?"

"And who is behind the notes, I wonder?" added Lorcan, rubbing his chin as he pondered the oddity.

"You don't think it's anything sinister, do you?" I tentatively asked, worry lines carving furrows into my brow.

"Poor Lily!" Andrea commiserated, "Not every mystery is going to turn up a new body or diabolical lunatic. You've had a time of it lately. I get it, but this sounds like a fun little prank and a possible riddle for some of us to decipher, no?"

"If you say so," I stated sullenly, "Just don't come crying to me if this turns out to be a lunatic Santa with a murder habit and a penchant for collecting things...like toes from his victims, or something."

"Toes?" Lorcan asked.

"Toes," I nodded my head, then groaned, leaning back, and looking at Andrea before finishing my thought. "What if this is the next hurdle in my horrid track record for making it to holiday celebrations? With my reputation, we could be searching for a serial killer or escapee from an insane asylum!"

"Well then," Andrea cried, "I guess we know what we have to do!" Lorcan and I glanced at each other then gave our full attention to my vivacious cousin as she continued. "We need to put our detective caps back on and solve this puzzle, proving to Lily that it's a fun caper and not a maniac on the loose! Oh, this is going to be fun! I know it!"

Didn't it usually go the opposite of what we hoped around here? I shuddered but didn't give voice to my misgivings. I could play this game; if it was a game, that is.

CHAPTER 3

"*F*riday morning, and all is well," I intoned in a whisper as I watched Hortense mix a potion in front of me. I stifled a yawn and tried to appear alert.

"Now, Lily. This concoction is an easy one for you to try on your own. Let's see how you do when mixing the ingredients." Hortense gave me an encouraging nod as I took the parchment from her hand. I glanced at the list and frowned when I made a note of the items I needed. Reaching for my small cauldron, with a pouring spout set to one side of the rim, I placed it on the smoldering coals in front of me then grabbed the first component.

"Wormwood? Uh, isn't that the main ingredient in Absinthe? Far be it from me to criticize the utilization of such an herb, especially since I am not remotely an expert on these matters, but isn't it highly poisonous?"

Hortense gave a little titter and caressed the pale silver-green herb before placing it in my hand. "Indeed, the compound found in Artemisia absinthium, thujone, in substantial amounts, can be toxic. However, we are using a minimal amount of this wormwood, and one cannot measure the benefits of my potion as a fever reducer, fearing an overdose. If my customers follow the instructions exactly as noted on the label, no harm will come to them. It is the same with any Western medicine warning; only my potion works!" She harrumphed.

Duly noted.

I placed the wormwood in the cauldron and added a few drops of lemon water, a teaspoon of elderberries, and a teaspoon of mugwort, another herb in the same family as the wormwood. It's purported to aid with colds and coughs. I finished with a bit of licorice root, anise, and peppermint. That was the easy part. Now I had to pick up my wand—I know, right? I totally get to use a wand—and stirred the contents clockwise three times while repeating the enchantment Hortense taught me:

> Starry night or sunny day,
> Make this fever go away,
> As the Moon returns to earth,
> As the Sun begins its birth,
> Dusk to dawn again times three
> Fever begone! Away from me!

A SLIGHT BLUE curl of sparkling smoke oozed out from the tip of my wand and wove its way around the top of the pot before dipping down and making a tiny poof before settling into the mixture. I carefully lifted the cauldron and poured the contents, now transformed into a dark purple liquid, into a waiting vial. Before I capped it, I held it in my hand, placed it up against my forehead where my third eye is supposed to be, and willed it to reduce all fevers. Then I carefully placed the little cork stopper in the bottle and let out the pent-up breath I didn't realize I was holding in.

"Very nice. It looks like you succeeded in this task, my dear. But now we need to test it on someone ailing. Let's see..." Hortense tapped her fingers across her lips and thought for a few seconds, much to my alarm. It was one thing making a potion and hoping I did well. Giving my concoction to an unsuspecting target, because, let's face it, I had an excellent chance of killing the poor soul, was downright criminal!

"Oh! I know. Doreen was telling me just yesterday that Donald was feeling poorly. She suspects he caught some bug when volunteering to drive the school bus since the usual lady called in sick. All those kids and germs, you know! Why don't you run it over to her now and try it out on him? He should be right as rain in twenty-four hours, a full three days if it is a nasty fever."

I looked in horror at Hortense while shaking my head no. Hermione came into the back room, all smiles, and agreed with her sister. "That's a great idea. You can bring her our new menu while you're at it. I just finished, and it has all our morning and early afternoon offerings for loose-leaf teas!" She proclaimed.

"No way! I love the Murphy's! Donald and Doreen were the first people I stayed with when I arrived in town. They let me have one of their motel rooms for pennies! And they fed me and even tucked me in at night. I can't do it. I won't! What if I kill him?" I cried.

Both sisters chortled and escorted me out of the back, placing the vial in a little decorative bag with their business card attached to it. Hermione made sure to add their new menu before sealing it.

"Nonsense," exclaimed Hortense, "You're overreacting! The worst you can do is make him break out in a pox or have him come down with a case of the chilblains. Those are the only two negative side effects when the spell is miscast. I am sure Doreen will call if he gets worse or keels over!"

With those words of encouragement, my confidence was even more wrecked as they ushered me out the door. The sisters urged me to go directly to my victim, um, patient's home, and have Doreen carefully follow the bottle's directions.

* * *

I WAS RIDING the high of successful potion-making. The outcome? My spell did indeed cure Donald, almost instantaneously. Doreen called the Winters sisters to tell them how pleased she was with me, and Hortense proclaimed me a brilliant pupil! Then I lost all my happy feelings and confidence upon entering my apartment. I breezed in the door and stopped short; Adriana was waiting for me. It was time for our lessons, but her countenance gave me pause, and I realized at once, something had made her upset.

"I didn't do it."

"Maybe you did." My great-grandmother peered at me shrewdly then shook her head in the negative. "No, probably not. You can barely find your way out of a cupboard. This has the machinations of someone diabolical."

Hey!

"I totally can pull off diabolical. Maybe it is me."

"No. It's not."

"Yes, it is."

"No. It's not. And stop trying to admit to something you couldn't possibly pull off."

"Yes, I could! Wait. What are we talking about anyway?" I was beyond confused at this point.

"We are speaking of this." Adriana thrust her hand out and

handed me a note that seemed suspiciously like the one that showed up on Lorcan's truck, my Uncle Stephen's café, and the Winters sister's shop. Only it wasn't because while it had the same cut-out letters glued to make a rhyme, this one was different. I took the note from my granny and began to read aloud:

THEY SAY A GIFT STRAIGHT FROM THE HEART
BRINGS GOOD TIDINGS TO THOSE FAR APART
BUT WHEN LOVED ONES ARE NEAR, AND FRIENDS
ARE CLOSE
THE GIFT OF TOGETHERNESS IS FAVORED
THE MOST
(No gifts necessary, but someone will get the prize!)

"WHAT THE HECK?" I reread it twice and still felt a nervous flutter in my belly. What if this was it? The evil asshat, here to ruin my Christmas. I did not want yet another trip to the hospital during a holiday. This was so not fair. Hold on. Why was this upsetting to my granny? It's not like anyone else who received a note had the misgivings I felt towards them.

"But...why are you upset? It's just a note. What gives?"

"What gives? What gives is that I've been up and down this town from one end of the square to the other. Do you know what I found?" Adriana was fuming as she paced back and forth, wearing a tread in my carpet. She was freaking out Wicked, who I just noticed was hiding under the loveseat, peering at the door to my apartment like it was an escape route she was contemplating acting on.

"Buildings and people in them?" I offered. An innocent expression was on my face as I tried to hide my smile.

My great-grandmother paused, hands on her hips, and gave me the stink-eye.

I instinctively felt the magic coming before she flicked her wrist at me and quickly blocked the magical head-thumping she sent in my direction. Instead, I countered, sending it bouncing away from me as if it were an annoying gnat. We both stared in shock at one another at my aptitude, then her cranky demeanor broke, and she smiled and nodded in satisfaction.

"You are learning! Buona, cara. Good!"

I stood there with a goofy grin on my face. I am not sure how I knew, but it just clicked.

"It felt natural...like...everything you've said over the last week made sense!" I gushed.

"I know you have it in you, kiddo. You just had to believe it and embrace it." Adriana stated. Then the frown came back in earnest, and she strode over to the recliner and sat, motioning that I should take the loveseat. I made kissy noises to Wicked, trying to draw her out from under it as I sat, but she just growled.

"To get back to what I am troubled about, and it is upsetting to me, so get rid of the attitude; it seems everyone I know received the notes that have circulated around town. But not me. I don't understand it. Why am I not invited to this thing?"

Oh. That's it then. It made sense why Adriana felt left out, but I was just surprised she wasn't suspicious of the intent behind these notes as I was and told her so.

"Why on earth would I be worried about a harmless puzzle? Someone is planning an event of some sort, but why have I been left out of it?" Adriana looked glum, so I didn't have the heart to tease her. That's my problem, I was too nice, as I'd been so recently informed.

"I'm a bit worried it might be someone wanting to harm,

or at the very least, is up to some mischief that could land me in the hospital again. Lorcan and Andrea seem to think I'm overreacting. Although, I didn't receive any of these notes, either. Where did you get those anyway?" I asked.

"They were on your truck, under the windshield wiper. You've been walking all over town lately. So, I guess you missed it!" My great-grandmother informed me, removing all sense of pleasure I felt in my witchy accomplishments a few moments before and sending a trickle of fear to the pit of my stomach. Was Adriana correct, and this was just a fun puzzle? Or did we all have something to worry about, and why was I the only one worried?

CHAPTER 4

I woke up at five Saturday morning to the sound of rain and a warm presence on my head that could only be my persnickety feline. That, and the fact that her tail was gently swishing back and forth across my face. Amazing how she had an abundance of attitude towards me yet always managed a snuggle in the middle of the night, purring softly and fooling me into a false sense of security.

I took some time to contemplate how I would move her off my head, knowing the last few times she managed to be up there resulted in a blood spill. My blood, with hurt feelings all around. Just as I was about to reach up and carefully pull Wicked down from her perch, she stood, did a full stretch on my noggin, and walked down my chest onto my stomach, where she promptly sat and began to wash. Seriously?

"As much fun as it appears you are having, Missy, I need to rise and go gather those ingredients Hortense entrusted I get for that potion she wants on Monday. Thanks to you, I won't be getting any extra sleep, it seems, so I might as well get up."

Wicked paused, and I noticed a bit of her tongue showing as she gazed over at me, listening to my words. It looked like she was sticking her tongue out at me, but I chose to believe it was just a hesitation in her washing and not her making fun of my plight, despite the malicious sparkle in her eyes.

What? I have an unusual cat. She truly understands everything that I say to her. We have a bond.

OK, maybe that was stretching it a bit, but she does have the uncanny ability to comprehend everything anyone says and acts accordingly. Leave it to the dark witch to have a magical cat.

Groaning in protest that even on my day off, I had a long list of things to do, I got out of bed and headed to the bathroom to get ready. I didn't take much time and grumbled as the cold air hit me, making my shower a quick one. Knowing today would be chilly had me choosing my clothing accordingly. It looked like a cold, rainy day was in order, so a sweater, jeans, warm socks, and an added knit hat for my head and hiking boots for my feet completed my ensemble.

I opened my apartment door and let out a blood-curling scream as I came face-to-face with Maureen Kennedy, June Carter's young assistant, standing in front of me holding a note.

"It's you! I knew these notes had to have some reprehensible intent behind it, and now I've caught you red-handed!" I shrieked.

"Um, are you mental? Like, I never fully believed Nora's claims, but you are certainly out there."

Oh, she could deny it and try to distract me by mentioning my unpleasant cousin, but it wouldn't work.

"Don't try to dissuade me, young lady...someone has been writing those freaky notes, and now I've caught you delivering one to my door. Why else would you be up here at this ungodly hour, skulking around?" I gave Maureen a smug smile.

It slipped a little when she responded, "Uh...because Ms. Carter heard you clomping around up here and thought to have me ask if you'd like some breakfast? I just got here and saw this on the floor and picked it up, then you opened the door and went all hissy-fit on me."

"That sounds like a made-up excuse!"

Maureen gave an indelicate snort and rolled her eyes.

"Look, go ask Ms. Carter. Seriously, I just arrived at your door. I wouldn't have time to write a note. And I wouldn't risk coming up the stairs and leaving it at your door if I was planning some weird trick or surprise on you. I didn't know you were getting any stupid notes. Maybe you have a secret admirer-or a stalker, more like."

"But..." I grabbed the note out of her hand and unfolded it. I quickly pulled it to my chest as Maureen leaned forward to read it along with me. Hmmm, she said 'to write,' as if she didn't know it was a cut and pasted one. That might be part of her ploy, or she might be innocent. In any case, I kept her prying eyes away from seeing it.

"Fine. I truly don't care what it says. If you want breakfast, Ms. Carter is making some." And with that, she stomped down the stairs, but not before I heard a mumbled, "freak."

With shaky hands, I reopened the note and read the message:

CAROL'S AND DANCING THE WHOLE NIGHT
THROUGH
GOOD TIDINGS APLENTY FOR ME AND YOU
BUT TIME FOR MERRIMENT SHALL HAVE TO PAUSE
WHEN THE HOUR APPROACHES FOR OLD SANTA
CLAUS

(Jolly Old Saint Nick should arrive 'round eleven...you've been warned!)

OH GOSH! Something terrible will happen at this stupid event; I was right! An evil Santa will descend and run amok on the square and start a killing spree of some sort.

Everyone I know and love will be there!

I flew down the stairs and into the small kitchen in the backroom of June's shop, June's Emporium. I found her pulling orange-cranberry scones out of the oven and smelled their heavenly scent, which almost sidetracked me into forgetting my mission. I opened my mouth to slander Maureen's already tarnished name when June raised her palm in the air to forestall my pronouncement.

"Before you impugn Maureen, know that I had to go pick her up very early this morning due to car trouble. It was just about five-thirty, and there was no note on my door. When I returned with her in tow, I found the third in the series, so there is no way it could have been Maureen. However, it does give me the willies that some unknown managed to get in the shop, or the back entrance at least, and climb your stairs, leaving a note outside your door." June worried her apron as she glanced at me with concern. Maureen watched us from the front room, and when she caught my glance, she curled her lip in a disdainful smirk.

"Unless we know who this person is, going around and leaving these notes, it's worrisome, no?" June fussed.

Finally! Someone else thinks these notes are somehow ominous!

"Thank you! I have been voicing my concerns on this very thing, yet everyone else seems to think it's all in good fun, and even Adriana is more upset she hasn't received any of them rather than how menacing they seem!"

"I didn't get one." Maureen pouted from the doorway. "I don't think it's such a big deal. It's probably just a prank to make everyone who gets excited about it seem like idiots." She said this directed at me, and I squinted, balling my hands into fists.

June glanced between the two of us and quickly ushered Maureen back into the storefront with admonishments to mind her business and not eavesdrop on personal matters. It was my turn to smirk at the insufferable girl when she tracked her eyes to me.

I even stuck my tongue out for good measure.

June returned to the kitchen, gently closing the door to the shop just as Wicked sauntered into the room looking for her breakfast. My cagey feline began purring the instant June came rushing over, offering sweet terms of endearment. It didn't hurt that June already had her dish outstretched as an offering to her goddess. Wicked even rewarded her with a head-butt to the chin, practically a sign of affection despite my knowing it was her way of having one lower their guard around her.

"You are going to spoil that cat with so much kibble. At the very least, you will make her fat."

Wicked raised her head, her intense green eyes piercing into my cognac brown ones as she stared, unblinking and intimidating.

"You don't scare me, cat." *Much.*

Sneezing in response, Wicked began to eat again fastidiously.

"I'm worried, June. I mean, on the surface, this doesn't seem like a dire situation. But with all that has been occurring lately, especially since I came to town, has me questioning the unusual and odd happenstance."

"Don't you go blaming yourself for every weird circumstance or random murder that happens around here, Lily. None of that was your fault!" I smiled at June's attempt to ease my consciousness, then flinched as she thrust a large brown bag at me. "Do me a favor and run this panettone over to your great-grandfather. I usually make them around this time of year, and he insists mine are better than your Uncle Stephen's. I refuse to comment further on the matter!"

That was wise. We had at least three phenomenal bakers in this town, my Uncle Stephen, June, and Joe over at the diner, and I wouldn't ever dare to proclaim who I thought was the best. You can't do the impossible, after all.

"Gladly, although he might be missing a small piece. It smells divine!" I peeked into the bag and noticed June had added a second loaf. They were delectable, sweet, yeast bread with citrine and raisins that was perfect with a hot cup of coffee.

"Don't you touch it! I have one right here with your name on it. Grab a slice and be on your way. Have you met Antonio's new nurse yet? She is a lovely girl who is..."

Just then, the bell sounded in the shop, and a deliveryman walked in, distracting June, so she didn't finish her thoughts. Waving me off, she bustled into the shop and left me to gather the panettone and my handbag and head out the door to my truck, George. I had a few books to return to the library today and knew I needed to make time to gather those ingredients to make Hortense's potion, and I had a lunch date with my friends. I tried to envision this new nurse great-grandfather had to aid him. I knew Andrea mentioned he was disgruntled at first, but now they had apparently become fast friends, and I wondered at his change of heart.

* * *

EVEN AS I pulled into the drive of Adriana and Antonio's whimsical yet stately Victorian, a shiver of Déjà vu overcame me. I remembered a tiny face gazing back at the home while my mom pulled away from the curb so many years ago now. Tears were in my eyes back then for having to leave a tiny black kitten I had found at a gas station behind, and I felt a few tears prick them now at the memory. I knew there was no way that little kitten and Wicked could be the same, but I did find it uncanny that she showed up at this same house then turned up at my family home on the same day. I chalked it off to an outré coincidence and a magical feline who decided to adopt me despite her snarky attitude with me.

I got out of my truck and headed up the steps, noticing how my great-grandparents went all out for the upcoming holiday. They had holly and a giant wreath on the front door and candles in every window. Antonio even strung those old-fashioned huge oval Christmas lights around the porch eaves and railings, and I knew I would have to drive by at night to see it lit up. I meandered around to the side porch and rapped a few times on the door before letting myself into the mudroom near the kitchen. I could smell the coffee before I entered the room and took a deep appreciative breath.

"Come in, come in. You must be Liliana! Hi, I am Keisha, Antonio's nurse." I shook the hand the young woman thrust at me while giving her the once over. I felt like I had seen her somewhere before, but I couldn't quite place her.

"Hello, yourself, and it's Lily. My great-grandparents keep using the name they insist my parents should have named me, and so far, I've let it go. However, I may start calling them Annie and Toto and see if they take the hint."

Keisha laughed, and that sense of familiarity came on again, yet I still couldn't come up with an instance where we might have met. Her dark hair was braided back and twisted up into a bun. Dressed in a simple grey sweater with jeans, she was slightly taller than me and petite. I looked on with envy at the bagel she had been enjoying, slathered in cream cheese, and wondered if her metabolism would rub off on me.

"Would you like coffee? Here let me take that panettone from you. If I leave it out, Mr. Antonio will get into it and finish it all before Miss Adriana can get a crumb, and this time, I think she'll spell him." We both laughed, and I agreed to a coffee when I realized of whom she reminded me.

"You don't happen to be related to Susanne Washington, do you? When you laughed just now, I saw something in your face that reminded me of her." I asked.

"You got the right of it. Susanne is my great aunt. My daddy is Doc Holcomb, her nephew. I should have introduced myself as Keisha Holcomb!" She smiled as we sat down at the worn oak table and began to doctor our coffee. "I heard all about your visit to my dad's office with your precocious kitty." She tittered.

"More like psychotic she-devil...and I am sure you did." I had just taken a sip of my coffee when Antonio shuffled in, and his face brightened when he spied me at the table. He was carrying a sizable ornate silver owl that he'd obviously been polishing. It was rather steampunk-looking with blinking lids that covered glass eyes and claws turned out so you could place a quill or other long item between them. The artist in me loved it in an instant.

"Liliana. Cara mia! Buon Giorno. Good day. You bring-a my panettone?" He asked, with his delightful Italian accent, while peering around the room inquisitively; at the same time, he leaned over to give me a peck on each cheek.

"Si, Grandpa...yes, but I don't believe I can tell you where Keisha has hidden it. I heard you gobble it up and leave crumbs for Great-Grandma."

My little gnome of a great-grandfather smiled widely, nodding yes.

"Where did you get that wonderful owl?" I asked.

"Gufo...owl. Si. Is belong to my mama. Ma I, how you say? I donato... ."

"Donate? Give?" I suggested.

"Si...donato. I geeve to town. Is sit on top pilastro near clock in square. I fix. I make shine." I deciphered the rest and understood that he donated his owl to the town, and it usually sat on a pillar in the town square near the big clock. Now that I thought about it, I did remember a small opening under the clock where the little bird could sit.

"I go feenish now." He patted my head and went to leave the room, but not before a crafty mien came over his face. "You no come inside. I wrap up you gift. You have café then andare subito, Liliana. Leave, OK?" He appeared a bit worried, and I hurriedly assured him I wouldn't peak into the other room. A look passed between him and Keisha as they shared a smile, so I gathered I must have quite the gift waiting for me in there. I needed to figure out what I was getting everyone for Christmas, and soon! He shuffled back into the adjoining room as Keisha promised him a slice of his special treat with some coffee once Adriana returned from wherever she had departed.

"Your great-granny hightailed it out of here early this morning acting all mysterious like. Adriana didn't realize I was already here on duty, and I walked in the foyer and found her getting ready to walk out the front door. I called out good morning to her, and she jumped straight in the air and spun around on me like a spooked cat!"

How odd. What on earth was she up to now? I found her skulking around highly suspicious and asked Keisha if Adriana explained her jumpiness.

"No...and I wasn't going to push the matter. She was spittin' mad that I caught her sneaking out the front door. I mean, that's what it seemed like to me. Adriana reminded me of Aunt Susanne when she gets caught coming back from playing bingo over with you Catholics on Thursday nights." We both laughed at the image, and I inquired about her aunt.

"How is Susanne? I hate calling her that, but she scolded me, saying it made her feel old. I need to make time to go visit her." Watching Keisha pick up her mug, I noticed a small notepad by her napkin. It jarred my memory of the mysterious notes popping up all over town, and I wondered if any had shown up here in the interim. "Oh, she is busy at her church and that choir of hers. They've been practicing all their hymns, and I think we will have a right special Christmas assembly this year."

"I heard you had some trouble with Antonio. He isn't too difficult, is he?" I worried that this pleasant young lady might have her hands full with my great-grandfather, but Keisha laughed off my worry and informed me they had worked out their differences. "Oh, he didn't like me coming in here and making him take his meds and restricting his diet. But we soon found out we have a lot in common. Both of us have a dark sense of humor and love a good practical joke. We even tweaked Miss. Adriana the other day, and for a minute, I thought I'd be in a heap of trouble, but she soon realized Mr. Antonio was happy and smiling and not complaining any longer—so I got a pass! I breathed a sigh of relief; let me tell you. I did not want to get on your granny's bad side!"

Smart girl.

I left soon after, made my way over to the park after querying Keisha, and found out that no mysterious notes had shown up. Maybe whoever passed them around town was intimidated by the aged pair of witches residing in the opulent Victorian.

I was relieved to find out Keisha and my great-grandad

didn't have any animosity toward one another. After meeting the young woman, I could tell that she could handle her difficult patient with ease, even with her slight frame. I wondered at their teasing Adriana, however. They may have to curb their shenanigans lest Granny, in her current mood, let loose a heap of wrath, putting a stop to their practical jokes. Of course, with Adriana fixated on others, she had less time to focus on me. And I could use a break!

Time to gather my ingredients.

CHAPTER 5

*A*fter a couple of hours trying to find ingredients, but only managing to find a half-dead herb, I decided to give up for the time being and go on to the next thing on my To-Do list, although this one was a more pleasant task— meeting my friends for lunch and gossip.

Martha Mosley, our town's new head librarian after the unfortunate demise of the former director, Edith Plank, was waiting for me outside the library, bundled up against the chilly weather. Edith was the latest murder to cross my path since moving to Sweet Briar and had even haunted me for a while before I solved her murder. Solved might be stretching it a bit because I just happened to be in the right place at the wrong time when it all went down.

Martha wore a beautiful woven scarf and matching knit hat, and a bright red jacket, very festive for the season. She waved when she saw me heading her way. I was picking her up and taking her to the diner to meet Becky Dolan, who owned The Reading Raven Bookstore, along with my cousin, Andrea. After the Edith fiasco, we had all become fast friends, and we were trying to decide whether to start a book club since we were all fans of mysteries. Becky and Martha have an endless supply at their disposal. Becky's shop had been open a couple of years now, and she just had renovations done when the Winters sisters took the adjoining shop for their tea and potions, connecting the two stores.

I pulled to the curb and watched Martha cross the street. Adriana and I still had to investigate the peculiar goings-on in her family—both her parents and an aunt died under mysterious circumstances. In light of what came out of the Edith Plank case, Granny and I suspected some tie-in and wanted to do some investigating—along with my family troubles—discovering the whereabouts of my dad and aunt. We'd decided to look into both matters in earnest but after the holidays. Martha gave me a bright smile and ran around the front of my truck before opening the passenger side door and hopping onto the bench seat.

"*Brrr.* It is cold out there today. I'm so glad you have the heater cranked!" Martha cried, warming her hands up against the vents under the dash.

I laughed and informed her George only had two settings, warm and hot, and the fan always stayed stuck on high, even if I turned the switch to low. Great in the cold winter, not so great in the Georgia humid summers, especially as he had no AC. I'd been kicking around the idea of parking him outside my shop and using him for advertising and getting a newer vehicle because I almost melted driving him around when I first got here, and that was September! I couldn't begin to imagine what July and August would be like!

I looped around the library, left my books in the depository, and then continued to my side of town. Parking at June's Emporium, the two of us crossed the street to Joe's Diner, where both Becky and Andrea were already seated at my favorite booth. As we entered, I was pleased to see

Shirley Jones at the register chatting with her sister Sheila, our waitress.

"Shirley! I haven't seen you for some time. How are you?" I asked the gregarious EMT who had patched me up on more than one occasion, the first being my second full day in town after Lorcan dropped me on my gravel driveway, where I'd landed on my head. Long story, don't ask.

"Look what the cat dragged in, Sheila! You staying out of trouble, Lily? No mysterious bad guys jumping out at you or bodies to trip over?" Laughing at her joke, I gave Shirley a droll look and replied, "Hardy har-har. You are a laugh riot. Bite your tongue before you jinx me, woman!"

"Oh, come now, ladies. I'm sure if we give it a couple more days, Lily will manage to get herself tied up in another nefarious situation with a body or two to complete the picture. I think she takes some perverse pleasure in finding them."

I inwardly groaned as I recognized the voice coming from behind me, not having to turn to see who was speaking. Brian. My ex-boyfriend, the police detective, managed to follow us into the diner. Turning, I was surprised to see he wasn't alone. A gorgeous brunette with almond-shaped eyes and light mocha skin was with him, her arm proprietarily wrapped around his. Yolanda Serrano, the medical examiner from Gwinnett County, I presume. She snickered at his jab and flung her honey-brown hair over her shoulder, giving me a not-so-subtle once over, and when finished, dismissed me with a delicate sniff.

I hated her on sight. I'm petty. *Sue me.*

It wasn't that I was jealous. Yolanda's catty attitude grated on my nerves, and I decided she was insecure about her status as far as Brian and she were concerned. Otherwise, there was no reason for her to be mean to me. I am wonderful. Just ask anyone. Or, well, maybe not.

I felt annoyed more than anything and had to bite my tongue. But as I stood there, I felt my magic kick on, but it was different than my usual dark coiling spiral coming up from the pit of my stomach. This magic felt like a warm glow, and I felt a sense of calm wash over me, along with what I can only describe as playful wickedness. Without even giving thought to what I was doing, I leaned into Brian and rested my hand on his arm.

"Brian! It is so nice to see you." Purring breathlessly, I slowly blinked my eyes, long lashes fluttering, and my mouth left slightly open after licking my lips, "You are looking well. You've shortened your hair a bit. I do prefer it longer."

As I spoke, I could see his nose flare and his pupils dilate a little as his eyes widened. He sucked in a sudden deep breath as Yolanda's eyes became slits. With that, I patted his arm and turned, sashaying slowly to join my friends at our booth, and took my seat—but not before flinging my long, glorious black mane over my shoulder for good measure. Peering over at Brian, I gave him a coy wink, then promptly dismissed him.

No one said a word at my table as Yolanda flounced by with a dazed Brian hurriedly following in the wake of her wrath. They chose a table as far away from us as they could, but I could still see Yolanda berating Brian through my lashes.

"Care to explain what that was all about?" Andrea asked as Martha and Becky shifted in their seat, mouths agog. "You are positively glowing and radiating this...this...intoxicating energy. I swear, you remind me of a cartoon character—one of those women with a long cigarette on a holder. You blow a puff of smoke that would coil toward Brian, caress his face and make that 'come here, big boy' finger motion. He's positively stupefied!"

"I don't know! Adriana has taught me to shutter my

emotions and add a glamor to project the mindset I'd like to display. I guess that woman's condescending attitude combined with Brian's rude comment flipped my witch switch on, and, voila! Wicked came out to play." I felt my magic draining, and my energy lowered to normal levels. Becky and Martha made knowing eyes at one another. Becky leaned forward and whispered her commentary so no one else would overhear.

"You just did sex magic, Lily. You all but cast a spell on poor Brian. I guess that's one of your abilities, and what an ability it is! You had better be careful around the opposite sex. Heck, even I feel a little flushed with that heady display of female wiles you just hit us with." Everyone chuckled as I looked on in alarm. "Brian keeps glancing over here covertly, but he isn't fooling anyone...especially that woman he's with." She finished.

Well, great. I think.

Sheila bustled over to our table with menus and asked if we wanted sweet tea. We all agreed to the South's official refreshment, and she rushed off to get our beverages.

I decided to ignore Brian and enjoy my lunch with my friends instead. Eventually, the topic turned to the mundane, mainly since I shut down any talk of my abilities. Thankfully everyone took the hint. I was touchy about it when you considered I didn't know my long list of talents, and I was embarrassed that Adriana was withholding them from me until I nailed the basics. I focused on what Andrea was saying and realized she was discussing the notes that kept popping up all over town.

Sheila came back with our drinks and overheard Andrea. "Hey! I found some tacked on my front door. They are driving Gordy nuts. He hates it when anyone litters, and he considers someone tacking paper up on your property littering." We all chuckled that Sheila's husband, the garbage collector, had a thing about trash. "Joe found them on the backdoor to the diner. He has been scratching his head, trying to figure out what it all means.

After taking our orders and getting them to Joe, who waved to us from the kitchen, Sheila returned to our table a few minutes later with our meals and some more news. "Joe said he saw someone skulking around town with what appeared to be paper notes in their hand. Could be he is an eyewitness to our Secret Santa prankster."

"Secret Santa?" I replied, "Why would you even consider it fun when it's anything but fun? I wouldn't say I like this. Not one bit." I protested then noticed the glances and sympathetic looks they were lobbing at me. "What?"

"Lily. You have gone through a lot these last few months, losing your mom and finding out about your life down here, that you are a witch. Then being attacked by Donna and that idiot Bubba after finding a skeleton under your porch and Chad dead on it." Martha commiserated. "Add Edith's demise and subsequent mess over at Nichols Pond, and it is quite understandable as to why you are cautious and unnerved by this."

"It sounds like a fun prank to everyone who's gotten a note. Honestly, why would someone send notes with evil intent to a town full of witches? Andrea asked. "I mean, they'd have to be insane to invite us to this Christmas Eve event, on the town square, and then try to do something to harm us!"

I chewed my bottom lip and met Andrea's gaze.

"What if they are drawing everyone out, giving a false sense of goodwill, and then attack with some massive spell?" I asked in a quiet voice, afraid of what my friends would think of me for being so paranoid.

Oh gosh. My friends were right. I was turning into my mother. Right here. I was sitting in my favorite booth at Joe's

Diner, hardly eating my juicy burger. I even ignored my fries, which is astounding for me, and spent most of the meal worrying my napkin to shreds. I've finally lost it. I was going mental. Paranoia would overtake me, and I would probably start hiding in my apartment and make excuses as to why I couldn't go out anywhere.

"Lily! There is no way you are going to become a hermit. We won't let you for one thing!" Andrea cried.

Oops. I let my ward down in my panicked state, and Andrea quickly read my mind. One of the first things Tanaquil, my dark magic teacher, taught me was to put up a block to stop other witches from scanning my mind. Once she showed me how to do it, I promptly became adept, although I still tended to slip up in moments of distress. This was one of those times.

"Stop it. Get *out* of my head."

Andrea looked abashed and quickly apologized. "I didn't mean to intrude. It was just so apparent that that's what you are worrying about, so I wanted to help. I'm sorry."

Now I felt like a louse for yelling at my dearest cousin.

"I'm sorry. I'm lashing out at you, but I'm agitated at myself for acting like my mom. All paranoid and nervous about this. Maybe you are all right, and I should ease up."

Martha and Becky sympathized but also informed me they were excited at having received the notes. OK, I could keep my feelings on the matter close and put on a happy face.

We were all about halfway through our meal when Jake came racing into the diner.

"Someone reported shots fired near the school!" Jake yelled, then spied Brian sitting in the back. "Brian, hurry...I can still hear them going off." Then he turned and ran back the way he came.

We all cried in dismay, and everyone stood up at once as Brian rushed to the front of the restaurant. I was just ahead of him and about to leave through the doors when I felt his hand grab my shoulder. "No, Lily. Please stay here. I can't concentrate on what may be going on out there if I know someone might harm you. Please. Just stay here. Stay down. All of you." He addressed this last comment to the room at large but then tracked his eyes back to mine and gave me a silent plea.

Whoa. I saw something there beyond the usual worry and knew I couldn't play at this man's heartstrings because despite how I felt about him, I could tell Brian had legitimate feelings for me. I slumped down in the nearest booth, and Brian hesitated just a second longer, then ran out into the street and towards the other side of the square to the middle school. Jake headed behind the first row of shops; the back of the school's administration offices lined the street just behind them, as did the school's playground portion. Brian was still on our side of the square.

I watched from the large window a second, then got up again and went out the front door to join my friends gathered at the curb. We watched as Brian made his way through the village green. The church bells were tolling the noon hour, and all the shopkeepers and a few townsfolk were standing outside, appearing confused and alarmed. We could now hear the sound of banging going off in the school's direction, but even I could tell at this point that we were dealing with fireworks of some sort. The explosions were crackling, and you could hear the whooshing sound of rockets.

I felt a hand on my shoulder and turned, finding Yolanda standing a bit too close for comfort.

"Yes?" I asked her, shrugging her hand from my shoulder.

"Let me make something very clear to you, dark witch or no dark witch. You aren't going to intimidate me or make Brian want to return to you. Especially not after he's been with me. So, you can forget playing games with his emotions."

OK, then. I opened my mouth to reply, but the lithe medical examiner pushed her way past my group and trotted across the street to the square, just as Jake and Brian were making their way over to us, dragging two young males who were kicking and screaming to be released. Jake was having a time of it, but Brian had a good hold of his quarry. I saw Lorcan rush over and help Jake, and the three men with the boys in tow made it to the sheriff's department and went inside.

"Well. What do you think that was about?" asked Becky, just as another voice cried out, "Hey, look at that!"

We scanned the area and spied a man standing close to the pharmacy, pointing up at the sky. Following his gaze, I was astounded to see two small planes with banners looping the airspace above the square, astounded because the flags were in the same fashion as our mysterious messages. They seemed just like the ransom notes with the same cut and paste lettering!

CLOCKS CLANG, AND FIREWORKS GO BANG!
NEXT TIME BUY THE BOOK, BUT HEY, MADE YOU
LOOK!

BOTH PLANES KEPT LOOPING in lazy circles around the village trailing their banners behind them. What on earth?

"What do you think it means?" asked Andrea excitedly, hopping a little as she continued to stare at the spectacle. "It's another message, but this one is...wow. I mean, someone hired two planes! What are the odds that we'd all be out here to see them?"

"Lousy. That's why someone planned this entire thing. Those weren't gunshots. You heard them," I complained. "We were drawn outside by firecrackers; they timed this perfectly. Those young men have some explaining to do. They are part of this tomfoolery, and now we've got them. Well, the police do, anyway!"

"I smell trouble."

We all jumped and spun at the voice that spoke right behind us. This voice coming out of nowhere business had to stop! I turned to find Stu Jones, Lorcan's mechanic helper standing behind us, pulling his lip and shaking his head.

"I don't like tricksters...and I smell one just as sure as I can smell a skunk. Trouble's a-brewin,' mark my words. Don't like fools who set off fireworks in broad daylight."

Considering that was one of the longest sentences I had ever heard Stu make, I took it to heart. At least I had another ally along with June. OK, so Stu might not be the brightest bulb on the Christmas Tree, but he sparkled in his own way. Um, maybe.

"Everyone thinks I am making too much over these notes and that they are harmless. What about you, Stu? You aren't happy with them. Have you gotten some too?"

Stu stood there a full minute, gazing at me without blinking. So much so that my own eyes began to tear up. I wasn't sure if he lapsed into a seizure or fell asleep with his eyes open, but I couldn't take it any longer. Just as I was about to wave my hand in front of his face to make sure he was still with us, he jerked his head back, then nodded yes. "Got three. Burned 'em all. I think it's the Devil's work." He turned and spit on the ground before squinting back at the four of us.

Andrea started laughing at this point and patted Stu on

the shoulder. "Oh, Stu. How can you say that? Why would the Devil invite us to a Christmas Eve party on the square?"

Stu's eyes widened, and he swallowed audibly then replied, "That's the question, now ain't it? Why indeed?"

Cue the spooky music. I just felt a goose walk over my grave.

CHAPTER 6

The excitement died shortly after that, and I drove Martha back to the library while Andrea and Becky headed back to their respective shops. Becky to her bookstore and Andrea to her dad's café. As I was looping around the square on my return trip, I spied Lorcan coming out of the sheriff's office. I honked, and he glanced up than smiled when he saw me pull over to the curb.

"Hey, stranger." He smiled then frowned when he heard a strange hissing sound coming from under the hood of my truck. "Do me a favor and pop open George's hood. I want to take a peek at him." Yet again, I inwardly smiled over Lorcan calling my truck by the name I'd given him. I hopped out and followed him around to the front and looked in. I was not too fond of the bit of smoke, hissing, and pinging sounds I heard under the hood and watched as Lorcan pointed to what appeared to be a ribbed black square.

"What is that?" I asked. "My radiator?"

Lorcan nodded yes and sighed. "I think you may need a new one. I was worried about it last time I did your oil change, and now I think it's going to be time to replace it."

"Ugh. I still have things to do. Now it looks like I will be walking."

"Where are you headed? I can take you." Lorcan suggested. I appreciated him offering to take me on my errands even though he had no idea what that entailed. But I knew he was busy at his shop with customers who wanted their cars checked before heading out of town for the holidays, and I said so.

"Don't worry. I have both Stu in today and Jack." Ah, his new apprentice. The one who helped me move my desk and other furniture up to my loft in the warehouse.

"I just saw Stu. He is fretting about the notes. See? I am not the only one who thinks they are evil. Stu agrees with me!"

"And you are proud of that, huh?" Lorcan chuckled.

"Hey... don't you go and put down Stu. He's my buddy. I can't help it if the rest of you can't see beyond the end of your nose. I am right, and I'm going to prove it."

Lorcan raised his eyebrows in surprise. "And just how are you going to manage that?" He asked.

"I am going to set a trap and catch the person in the act. That's how!"

Lorcan groaned. "Somehow, I knew you'd say that."

He climbed in my truck, and we drove to his garage, where I pulled George into one of the empty bays. On the way over, he informed me the two young men who set off the fireworks were none other than the Kowalski twins, Alex and Bart. I had briefly considered them suspect on the Edith Plank murder case, but things came to a head before my snooping brought me in contact with them. Both brothers were constantly in and out of trouble and gave Sheriff Glen grief weekly.

Lorcan explained, "They professed their innocence on being behind the notes, and Brian and Glen concurred with their proclaimed innocence. Both boys said they found a bag of fireworks in the bed of their truck with a mysterious note that stated they didn't have the guts to set them off at noon in the schoolyard, complete with a big, fat 'dare you!' attached. Plus, Alex informed us, 'shucks, we never back down from no dare!' Not that I wouldn't put it past the two, but when the notes started appearing a few days ago, both boys were with their mother in Atlanta visiting their ailing grandfather. So, they have an alibi."

I opened my door and sighed, reflecting on George, and I gave him a fond pat when I got out. I hope he made it through the winter. Even though I had a little nest egg, I didn't want to splurge on a new vehicle right now. I knew, come spring, I would be knee-deep with home repairs and renovations.

After giving Stu and Jack instructions for the rest of the afternoon, Lorcan grabbed the keys to his Chevy, and we were off.

"So, where is it we are heading?"

"The woods. Any woods. Well, maybe not the one where Nichols Pond is. However, I've been back and tried calling out to whoever was in the water. She doesn't surface. Maybe I dreamed it." I lamented. I went at least four times at first in the hopes of seeing the water sprite or mermaid. I still wasn't quite sure what she was. It wasn't like she had a tail or anything, but no way could a human live at the bottom of a pond and remain under the water as long as we did. I was grateful she helped me breathe and wanted to understand why she was there and what those pearls meant to her—another puzzle to add to my list.

"Well, why don't we go to the woods west of town near Bear Gap Mountain? Just what do you need to find anyway?"

"The Winters sisters have me making potions and gathering ingredients. I'm not supposed to cheat and rush over to

Samantha and have her hand them over to me. So, I need to hunt them down and bring them to Hortense on Monday. After that, I want to plan out how I'm going to nab this prankster and save the town."

Lorcan didn't say anything right away, and I suspected he too thought I was overreacting. We sat through an awkward minute of silence, and then he sighed and glanced over at me.

"Lily..."

"I know. I'm ridiculous. You can't believe how stupid I am."

Lorcan gave me a weighted look, and I braced myself for the onslaught of reprimands that he would lob at me for daring to try and catch a nutcase on my own.

"First of all, I would never call you stupid. Ever. Second, you have gone through so much since you've been here, and I know you've built up in your mind the expectation that somehow soon, in some way, and by some unknown, you will have something happen that will have you spending Christmas in the hospital, or worse." Lorcan stated, and his kind brown eyes flicked back over to me again, then back at the road. "And that's why..."

"That's why you think..."

Lorcan stopped me from further interrupting him by talking over me. Loudly.

"That's why I am not going to let you go investigating alone. I will be right there with you, helping nab the culprit."

I was rendered speechless. Me. I had so many thoughts running through my head, but the most predominant one? How the heck did I wind up with such a good friend in Lorcan? Wait a minute. He was just saying that, so he didn't have to admit he thought I was a scatterbrained nutcase. I just knew it.

"You aren't a nutcase, Lily." Oops! Even with my witchy instruction going strong, I tended to forget to shield myself from having my mind so easily read during times of emotional duress.

I scowled, and Lorcan chuckled.

"I'm sorry. I didn't try to read your mind, but you are an open book at the moment."

I adjusted my thoughts and put up my wall, then turned towards Lorcan and continued, "You don't have to go to the trouble of humoring me and losing time at your business just to cater to my whims...or neurosis." Great. Before I'd moved down to Georgia from New York State, my mom and I had garnered a reputation as the town loony's, thanks to my mother's penchant for believing any and every conspiracy theory known to man. She also covered all our windows in blankets and wouldn't dream of owning a credit card or using a cell phone, not that she could have afforded one. I already have a portion of the townsfolk looking askance at me for being a dark witch. I didn't need lunatic tacked on.

I slowly breathed in then let it out, "I appreciate the offer, and if I decide to go hunt this person or set a trap, I promise you will be the first person I call to help."

"That's all I ask."

"You know, I am a dark witch. I can take care of myself. Heck, I did take care of myself before I even knew I was a witch. I am learning to control my powers too, so let's not discuss the last time we tried to take on the baddies together." I griped.

Lorcan tipped my chin up, forcing me to look him in the eyes.

"I don't doubt you. At all." Lorcan affirmed.

"But..."

"But...I would sleep better at night knowing you were planning to call me to be your partner in crime and not worry about you out there with a possible lunatic to catch."

"Wait. Do you agree with me? You think this person

creating these notes could be dangerous?" I asked incredulously.

"Well, no. I'm not going to lie and tell you I feel as you do. I think this is harmless. As a matter of fact, I think this is someone who is planning something that we will all enjoy and is having fun spinning our wheels. Nefarious intent? No. I tend to get alarm bells going off at times, and my alarm bells are silent."

"Yeah, well, maybe they are broke. Or the batteries ran out." I countered.

"Nah. I'm hardwired. If I'm not getting woo-woo feelings about these notes, you can take it to the bank that the person or persons behind them are benevolent."

Then why did I feel like something awful was about to happen to our little town?

We spent a good hour gathering the ingredients I needed for Monday, even though I had to rely on Lorcan's expertise. Everywhere I looked, I encountered weeds and dead vegetation. Everything appeared the same to me, and I cursed my luck at not learning potions and herbs in the spring and summer when everything would be in bloom.

Afterward, Lorcan suggested an early dinner a few towns over in Hiawassee, where we decided on southern BBQ in the form of ribs, baked beans, and pink lemonade at The Happy Hawg on Lake Chatuge. Later we wandered over to Towns County Park and the Hamilton Gardens trails to work off our filling dinner. Even though it was chilly and darkness was coming on quickly, Lorcan and I enjoyed walking down to the lake and watching folks bringing their boats up the ramp as they headed home for the evening. Suddenly, I jolted and pulled Lorcan back the way we had come from, then yanked him behind a large Magnolia tree.

"What's wrong, Lily?"

"Shh!" I hissed, "Look over there to your left. Isn't that

Dennis Carter, and if I'm not mistaken, it's not June he's with, but Rita Chase again. And over here where no one from our town can find them out!"

I frowned in distaste at the pair and couldn't believe Dennis would cheat on June with Brian's mother. Jake hadn't said anything, but a few weeks past, I noticed his face darken when his dad and Rita's name came up as being together—albeit innocently having breakfast with Samantha Fairburn in tow—at my Uncle Stephen's café.

"This doesn't look good."

"I don't know what to think," Lorcan groused. "I mean. They aren't kissing or anything. It appears they may be breaking up. Isn't Rita crying?"

Now that he mentioned it, it did seem as if Rita was sobbing, and Dennis was comforting her as best he could. He was on one knee in front of her, peering up at her face. Suddenly, Dennis stood and sat on the bench Rita occupied and put his arm around her, pulling her to his shoulder. Then he placed a kiss on the top of her head and patted her back over and over.

"She is definitely upset about something, that's for sure. And so far, nothing they are doing looks like a lover's spat, but what in heavens name are they up to?"

"I'm not sure," Lorcan replied, "but we need to head back to my truck before they spot us, and it gets uncomfortable fast."

I almost wanted that to occur. At least I'd have answers and could decide if and when I should say anything to Jake. Or June.

We reached Lorcan's truck, and I climbed in but kept peering over to where I could still make out the couple. They were still in the same position, and I grumbled my frustration. "I don't like this, Lorcan. I know I should stay out of it. But June is my mother's best friend. My friend. If I don't say something, and she finds out? Worse if she found out I knew about it and didn't say anything to her? I am afraid our friendship might come to an end."

"You need solid evidence, Lily...think of how bad it would be for everyone involved if this was something innocent that appeared bad...and all the hurt that would follow in its wake if you did say something!" He had a point.

Just as we crossed the bridge back into the central part of town and onto the road that would take us back to Sweet Briar, I cried out and pointed to an older green Lincoln Town Car and, more specifically, the person behind the wheel, that has just passed us on my right.

"What on earth is my great-grandmother doing way over here? She didn't see us, but I was able to gaze down at her from up here, she has a car full of shopping bags, and if what I think I just saw is true, they are all from an office supply store!" My eyes widened as realization set in. "Lorcan! What if she is our note maker? That would explain why she snuck over here and went to an office supply store and not the one closer to our town! I knew there had to be someone reprehensible behind all this. And you can't get more diabolical than Adriana Dolce!"

CHAPTER 7

The rest of the weekend went by quickly, and I found myself back at potions lessons with the Winters sisters bright and early on Monday. Well, it would have been bright if they could have kept the rainclouds at bay. They hadn't. It was currently raining buckets, and I was wringing my hands as I awaited Hortense's verdict on my potion-making assignment that I'd completed late last night.

I'd left several messages for my great-grandmother, but she hadn't yet returned my calls. Grandfather Antonio informed me she had been visiting a sick friend at a tardy house and was staving off doors by lying with a rebel tornado. That's what his explanation sounded like since it was half in English and the other in Italian, of which I was hardly proficient. When I asked him if she had been shopping, his reply left me even more confused, "Si, she go...andata...ma perché se gelosa...she need to create some ah, eh no, she no get. You no worry. Everything good. Buona. Hai capito cos'ho detto?" Um, everything was good because a ho has debt? Sure. We'll go with that. Whatever he said.

Hortense proclaimed my potion a success, and she

asserted I was a marvelous pupil sending me over to work with Hermione next. Both Hermione and my great grandmother had been switching off my Basic Witchcraft: Spells and Incantation lessons. Today happened to be Hermione's day on, which was reasonable in light of Adriana going AWOL. I secretly preferred Adriana but would never admit it lest her head puff up to epic proportions with my revelations.

I quickly learned all my elemental spells and had even impressed myself with how easily I seemed to comprehend how to perform each one and do them effortlessly. Until the new year, the following few lessons would still be the basics but advanced. Stuff that would require a proficiency level that, once mastered, would put me on the same level as other adult witches. My instructors felt I was ready, and surprisingly, I did too! I only managed to mess up on the rare occasion I rushed ahead on a spell or didn't accurately execute it, usually due to my being distracted or not having listened to the instructions correctly in the first place. I blamed this on everyone forcing me to keep early hours.

Today Hermione was in a severe mood, rare for her.

"Last week, you graduated from adept to advanced...so today we will improve on your technique and crafting footprint. Each witch has their way of personalizing the basic spell sets. It is similar to handwriting in cursive. We all learn how to do it, but everyone has their own unique type, like a signature. When you find yours, it will be your calling card. Once the spell is cast, everyone will know it was one of yours by the branding you impart. This is not true of dark magic. That is why it is so dangerous and, while not forbidden, per se, is cautioned amongst covens. If it were easy to trace a dark witch by their spellcasting, we would have been able to track down your father and aunt by now.

"The magic used to cloak them was dark...and while we

may have been able to follow some of the trails, any dark utterances to confuse or hide would have us running in circles, or worse...entangling us in the web. You can see why your family was thrilled to have you back! You show promise, one who can decipher the personal code another dark witch casts. Why, if that is the case, you, my dear, might very well be instrumental in finding your kin!" She declared, leaving me with my mouth hanging open. I had no idea that I even had that ability and realized she just let me know one of the purported seventeen I possess.

"Do you truly believe I could track them, Hermione?" I enthusiastically inquired.

"I don't see why not, Lily. You are a powerful witch."

"Teach me. Please?" I suddenly had all the motivation I needed to toss my aspersions to early morning lessons, along with grumbles that I had to learn so many spells. I focused on everything Hermione imparted in the next hour.

Sixty minutes later, my mind was reeling with everything I'd learned that morning, and I was completing my last task, trying to trace the patterns in a spell cast by Adriana that was very dark and potent magic. I didn't realize it was she who cast it until I was halfway through my analysis. I'd diligently gone from tracing to tracing until I saw a tiny purple aura that pulsed brighter than my tracking magic. I sat back, astounded that I could distinguish one from the other, and then it dawned on me where I had seen that purple pattern before.

"This is Adriana's work!" I shouted, earning a wide grin from Hermione.

"And how do you know this?" She asked.

"Because for the last few weeks, she has been leaving little surprise magic spells behind to scare the living daylights out of me when I was least expecting them. Remember the eyebrow incident? Adriana. The exploding stinky blasts in my truck? Adriana. The fact that for four straight days, every time I tried to enter Joe's Diner or my Enchanté Café, I'd get blasted with a mini-tornado, resulting in a bad case of bedhead? Adriana.

"I didn't grasp it, but each time the color purple was just barely evident, glowing and imprinted if I bothered to look close enough at the remnants of the spell. I didn't because I knew Granny was behind each. But had I done so? I would be miles ahead of where I am right now. Lesson learned!"

I knew my own magic cast blue tints and had seen the same in Adriana's, but hers were darker and more indigo, to purple. Could it be so easy? I asked Hermione.

"For the average witch, tracking can be relatively easy. But whenever a dark witch casts a spell with malicious intent, the task falls to Trackers—specially trained witch's adept in all forms of magic. But even they have a difficult time, and as I said, run the risk of becoming tangled in the magic the evil witch who cast such spells left behind. You seem to be unaffected by these remnants. So, I am going to go out on a limb and declare you a superior Tracker. They are called Shadow Dancers. You, Lily Sweet, are the strongest I've ever beheld."

Wow. I like my new superpower. It was way better than the Inept-A-Girl I had dubbed myself recently!

Hortense and Hermione sent me off with matching beaming smiles to my next lesson, this one at the charming cottage around the corner from my family home, which belonged to my dark arts instructor, Professor Snape. No, I jest.

Tanaquil Alessi, Elder at our Council of Witches and a teacher of the Arcane Arts, lived around the corner from my future home in a darling shotgun cottage. The theory is, you could stand at the front door and shoot a gun, and the bullet would travel through the house and out the back door without so much as making the curtains flutter. I loved it at first sight. I also was rather fond of Tanaquil after our tenuous introduction a few weeks ago at my witchy ability testing fiasco.

She was a formidable teacher who knew her stuff. Tanaquil appeared to be a miniature version of Reba McEntire threw me for a loop every time I saw her. And I had to peer far down while doing so. A quick perusal of Wikipedia imparted upon me that Ms. Reba stood at five foot seven inches tall. Tanaquil was almost a head shorter than me. I am five foot three, and if she were a tick over five feet, I'd eat my shoe. Heck, if we tussled her hair, and she came in at four foot eight, I'd eat it. She was delicate, almost frail-looking. Like an ethereal red-haired fae creature, petite and graceful...one of Tinkerbell's friends I'd seen on the Disney Channel.

Today I had a tagalong buddy attending class with me. Because upon entering my truck outside the Winters' shop, I was startled to find Wicked curled up on the passenger seat, asleep. How she got into George without thumbs was beyond me because his windows weren't left open, not in this rain. She was dry and warm and barely glanced at me as I climbed in and started the engine.

"Are you going to tell me how you got in and why you are here? No? Well, I won't be carrying you into Tanaquil's home. You can forget that, so you can spend the next hour snoozing away, Missy." I informed her as I opened my door and got out.

I settled into the armchair in Tanaquil's study, Wicked in my arms, as my instructor bustled in with a tray laden with tea and goodies.

"Such nasty weather. Are you cold? I could light a fire if you'd like." Not waiting for a reply, Tanaquil snapped her fingers at the hearth with a soft command, 'flame,' and the logs ignited. The pleasant smell of wood smoke quickly filled the room. That was a handy trick. I wondered what would happen if I snapped my fingers. No. I glanced around the room filled with its old books and delicate wallpaper and thought, perhaps not. Especially with my track record. Although it did make my fingers itch to give it a try.

"Hello, darling." She cooed.

I went to reply with a bemused come back when I realized she was talking to my cat. My smile slipped.

"Now, where are we in our studies?"

Before getting into lessons, I thought to tell her my concerns regarding my great granny's odd behavior and suspected perverse doings around town. I explained my worry that she might be our culprit and up to some mischief by spreading the notes. I worried at Adriana's mental state, especially by pretending to be offended that no one had sent her any of the puzzles.

"You don't think she's...um...off her rocker, do you? I mean, I've joked before that the family may want to consider sending her away to a happy retirement home for deranged old witches, but no one is listening to me."

Tanaquil, laughing in an enchanting way, like tiny bells trickling across the room, responded.

"Oh, I think she is wonderful. I also don't believe it is she who is spreading these notes."

When I asked Tanaquil to elaborate, she instead gave me an enigmatic smile and suggested we concentrate on lessons rather than speculations and intrigue.

Ouch.

"OK, then. What's on today's agenda?" I asked. "I believe we ended last week discussing hexes and why we never use them."

"Right. Well, this week, I think I'd like to delve a bit darker in your instruction, my dear. I feel you are at a disadvantage when under attack, and you do seem to draw your fair share of negative forces and those with evil intent. It's time you learned how to deal with them. Now, I have heard how you dispatched Beau Buford, but I suspect that was a purely instinctual response to being in the situation and the heat of the moment, so to speak, that ring you wear surely aided you. I've noticed you do not wear much else except for that charming necklace and matching ring. Sweetbriar roses! How delightful. Our town's namesake."

I stroked the tiny rose charm I wore around my neck, then down to the ring that I found at the bottom of Nichols Pond. I hesitated to mention the incident to Tanaquil, or anyone really, that a water nymph of some sort led me directly to it. What if they were to bring her harm? I felt indebted to the creature for saving my life, after all. It wasn't like I would have been able to hold my breath and reach the bottom and get back to the surface without running out of air. Heck, I did run out of air, and the gracious water sprite breathed for me. If that wasn't saving my life, I don't know what is!

"Tanaquil, not to go off subject or anything," I began worriedly, "What other magical beings are out there? I mean, there can't just be witches and the occasional ghost. Now that I am aware of the paranormal, I assume there are other beings?"

I held my breath as I saw conflicting emotions cross Tanaquil's face, wondering if she'd humor me by satisfying my inquiry.

"Lily. Before I reply, let me inform you that many of the mythical beings in stories and movies you have grown up with left you with preconceived ideas, not necessarily based on fact. That said, many of them are, indeed, real."

"Not to go all Twilight on you...but we are speaking about

vampires and werewolves and the like?" I managed to squeak out.

"Not to get all Twilight in my response, but yes." She replied.

OK, then.

"What about water creatures like, um, mermaids?" I tentatively asked.

"You mean like Ariel? No, dear. No Little Mermaids are running around singing about getting a pair of legs." Tanaquil smiled at me, and I deliberated how I'd ask about my water woman when she continued. "Unless, of course, you are speaking about water witches, which go under the more common name of sirens. They, indeed, are real and have been a thorn in our side for millennia. Their historical intent has always been to sway humans, men more so than women, into doing their bidding with their enchanting voices. As generations have passed, factions have broken off where the majority are now benevolent and keep a low profile. Occasionally, a rogue siren will use her voice as a weapon and ensnare an individual. Or try to topple nations. They are usually hunted down and eradicated."

Eek.

That certainly didn't make me feel comfortable enough to mention my encounter with what I now believed was a siren in Nichols Pond, especially when remembering how her eyes had turned black as mine did, which means what? Probably that she was a dark siren as I was a dark witch. However, I had a feeling they might have more definite beliefs in the evilness of their dark sirens than what it meant to be a dark witch in our world. Oh, well, just great.

"Do vampires and the like ever show up in town? I mean, is it something I need to worry about or plan for the eventuality of?" I asked. Part of me had hoped Tanaquil would have laughed out loud and assured me we were the only paranormal beings on the planet, the other half kind of expected this news, but I didn't have to be happy about it.

"We had whispers of one a long, long time ago. Georgia isn't a hotbed of vampire activity. We tend to get countless ghosts and see a Geisterjäger's come through town every few years. Oh, and I saw a demon once; I chased him off, though. Our town is pretty calm as far as the paranormal. I have been teaching you how to defend yourself. You will be fine. One of my lesson plans will go over what spells to use on what monster or some such, so you can handle anything you come across." She stated indifferently. She was so blasé about it that my nerves calmed a bit, however unnerving this news was.

"What the heck is a Geisterjäger?" I dared ask.

"They are ghost hunters from the Old Country...although there are quite a few family's that hunt in the United States. I think one family is in Charleston, South Carolina, and another somewhere north of us in Tennessee."

Then Tanaquil's previous words filtered through my brain.

"Hold up a minute. You said demon. Like the Devil? I'm about to go running for the hills!"

Tanaquil laughed aloud at my look of alarm and quietly did her best to reassure me.

"These are lesser demons who also hunt ghosts. Well, lost souls anyway. Suppose a Geisterjäger fails on their mission to convince a ghost to move on, or worse. In that case, if one of their ghosts turns into a poltergeist, which usually happens due to extreme situations and conditions, a demon will swoop in and steal that soul, claiming victory. Geisterjäger's and demons are mortal enemies, you see."

I see. Geisterjäger's sounded a bit like a Tracker. So, I mentioned to Tanaquil how Hermione had proclaimed me a Shadow Dancer, and she didn't seem at all surprised.

"Yes, dear. It's one of your talents."

"Do you know what all of them are?" I squeaked out excitedly.

"No. I just got off the phone with Hortense before you arrived, and she was gushing about your lesson today. She had nothing but praise for you and mentioned your tracking abilities. That's how come I know. Very good I'm pleased for you. However, we are taking time away from today's lesson, so I suggest we continue."

Right. Let's get cracking on my lessons. We spent the next two hours going over attack and defense spells, and I was rather pleased with how adept I was becoming with these lessons. Perhaps, come spring, I might be able to graduate to the highest level of spellcasting. Tanaquil agreed that I was getting the basics down, which had me wondering if a word or two from her to Adriana might get me a glimpse of what the rest of my long list of supposed talents were. The only other person who knew was Olivia Ogden-Meyers, and I wasn't about to ask Brian's great aunt, herself an imposing witch, to go against Adriana's wishes and spill the beans. Yet.

Speaking of Adriana, my nose was out of joint because she finally called but only to inform me something had come up and she wouldn't be able to do my lessons today and the next few days. Moreover, she refused to answer any of my questions as to why. Oh, really? Could it be that my demented imp of a granny was plotting her next move? Perhaps a mysterious note campaign? It was time for a stakeout!

CHAPTER 8

*F*or the next two nights, I staked out areas around the town to no avail. No crazy old woman was running amok in the streets, no notes showing up with further cryptic messages. Nothing. I was dragging at lessons every morning that followed and was now sequestered up in my loft at Found Things, my art studio, with Jake, Lorcan, and Andrea watching me pace while I pulled on my hair.

"She has to be plotting her next move and probably saw me hiding in the shadows. I don't know what I can do to entice her out into the open, so I can expose her for the crazy loon she is. The town will proclaim me a hero for capturing such a menace, and after carting her off to the asylum, I will be handed the Key to the City. I know it."

All three of my friends were laughing so hard by the time I finished my diatribe that Stu walked in from next door, scratching his neck with a wrench, and peered up at the four of us, then shook his head and headed back to the mechanic shop. His antics just set everyone off even more and caused me to fall even deeper into a pissy state. I sat on my chair in a disgruntled heap and gave them all a sour look.

"Go ahead and laugh. I know I am right about this. I just have to figure out how to catch Adriana at it." I stated.

Lorcan raised his hand as if asking for permission to speak, his shoulders still rocking with laughter.

"As much as I am enjoying following you around in my truck to keep an eye on you, I am losing sleep... it's getting beyond chilly out there, and don't you think perhaps she is on to you if she's our culprit?" He asked, then ducked when I tossed a polishing rag at his head.

"You were the one who told me to call you so you could watch over me and keep me safe...not that I think I need watching. I don't need anyone helping me either. I can set a trap for the old hag and catch Adriana red-handed!"

"Not that I even remotely think she is behind the notes," Jake started. "But don't you suppose that, perhaps, she is cloaking herself as Andrea does?"

Hey now! Wait a minute!

"That's brilliant, Jake! How come I didn't think of that? Andrea, do you know if Adriana can cloak herself? Is it one of her abilities?"

Andrea scrunched up her face and thought for a minute, then shook her head no. "I'm not sure. I mean, Granny is talented. She can do a plethora of spells and incantations. So, I wouldn't put it past her, but I don't know for sure. However, that doesn't matter now, because duh! Lily. I can cloak you! I can't believe I didn't think of offering my help with this. When you told me, I was relieved that Lorcan would be with you and you wouldn't be alone out there in case..."

Andrea didn't finish her thought, and I suspected she was going to wax poetic about my inability to cast a proper spell. She blushed and glanced down quickly as my eyes moved to hers, and I squinted.

"You don't have any faith in my abilities...none of you,

even after two solid weeks of instruction with amazing teachers and me being this all-powerful dark witch. I will have you know Hortense and Hermione think I am brilliant. I have made two potions already, on my own, and one of them has completely cured Donald Murphy of a nasty cough. Tanaquil was so impressed with my lessons this week that she told me I would be a force to be reckoned with come springtime."

I could see by their faces that my dearest friends doubted my proclamations, if only slightly, but it still stung. OK, so I embellished a little there at the end. But I was confident I would be beyond adept when flowers were blooming again and butterflies were flitting to them. I hoped, anyway.

"I know...look at what I learned on Monday!" I stood quickly and pointed to a pile of paper towels crumbled on the floor below that I had used to clean varnish off an old wood and rattan rocking chair. Raising my hand, I mimicked what I witnessed Tanaquil do, and snapping my fingers in the directions of the paper, I stated in a loud voice, "Flame!"

* * *

THE FIRE DEPARTMENT assured me I wouldn't need to call my insurance company because the only damage had been to the rocker, which was now a pile of ash on the concrete floor. I assumed the paper towels instantly evaporated from the intense heat, and not a trace of them would ever be found, even in the cracks and crevices. The fire chief stated he was thrilled the structure's foundation, made of extra-thick concrete and high ceilings, prevented the fire from spreading. I was still upset Jake had rushed to call them, mainly since there was a hose in the alley, and we had it under control by the time the fire truck showed up with my favorite deputy following closely behind. Not.

Officer Delaney was only too happy to write me a citation for starting a fire in an enclosed structure without a permit or any common sense. Yes. He actually wrote that on the ticket. Before he could hand it off to me, Jake grabbed it and stared him down when he started posturing that I might need to come down to the station to explain casting spells without supervision or ability. That stung too. I was about to show him just how happy I would be to continue casting spells when Brian walked in and sent the deputy packing.

He also sent the gawking crowd on their way, but most of the bystanders were reluctant to part, it seemed. I guessed most of them were hoping for a second act. I did catch some sympathetic smiles from June, Sheila, and Joe. Even Stu gave me a thumbs up as if to say, 'it will all be fine,' that or he was a closet pyromaniac, and I'd given him a thrill with my performance.

"What were you thinking?" Brian pulled me aside despite glares from both Jake and Lorcan and a sneer from Andrea. I didn't want my friends to give him their attitude just because we had broken up or I had pulled away from any relationship we might have had. It wasn't fair to Brian, who was a good friend to them before I'd arrived. So, I gave them all my best frown as Brian led me into the alley between the shops.

"I wasn't thinking, I guess. I wanted to show everyone that I could perform spells but forgot that Tanaquil had used a soft voice when she uttered the command in front of me this week." I felt miserable and must have looked the same because I could see the intense scowl wither from Brian's eyes replaced with one of sympathy and a bit of mirth.

"Lily, what am I going to do with you?"

I wouldn't say I liked the sound of that, not coming from Brian, and especially not after seeing the raw emotion in his eyes when he gazed at me and thought a shooter might be on the loose in town last week. I'd also noticed he hadn't begged

Yolanda to stay safely inside and not get in harm's way so he could concentrate on the task at hand. I knew Yolanda noticed and could still feel her nails digging into my arm as she warned me to keep my distance.

Ugh. I had to stay strong and not react when Brian peered over at me like a lost puppy who found his home. Mostly since there was still a tiny part of me thrilled that the cool guy, not to mention a freaking gorgeous specimen of male perfection, wanted me. I even had little teenage flutters of electricity go through me whenever I saw him around town. This close, and I knew I had to thrust my brain forward and move my heart and any other, ahem, girl parts to the background, lest I fall under his winsome spell again.

Did I mention he smelled like standing in the forest while gazing out at the ocean at twilight?

I bit my lower lip and stepped back even as Brian gave me a knowing smile. "You don't have to worry about doing anything with me, thank you. Shouldn't you be handling crowd control or something? I'm sure everyone standing around outside is causing quite the traffic jam." I made little shooing motions with my hands, but he just chuckled.

I jutted my chin out and tried to appear calm and collected but couldn't hold his gaze. I needed to work on that. Brian didn't close the distance I had made between us but did reach out to tilt my chin up, making our eyes connect again.

"Don't worry about the citation. Tell Jake he can toss it. I will talk with Deputy Delaney and ask him to stop harassing you for ridiculous reasons. Nora is back and living with him now. Did you know that?"

The look of shock on my face was all the answer he needed.

"Just be careful around them both. Nora seems to be up to something. I am afraid her animosity towards you has multiplied instead of the opposite. I will try to keep her from bothering you, OK?" Brian reached out and tucked a strand of hair behind my ear that just happened to be one of the purple streaks I sported, then smiled, albeit sadly, turned and walked out of the building.

Oh, yes. I certainly needed to guard my heart against any feelings that man brought up and out of me, especially as I had more important things to consider in light of what I just learned. Because now I had a second suspect to add to my list. Cousin Nora. She could easily be behind the mysterious notes and plotting some sinister prank on those I hold dear. And with the help of her boyfriend, one Deputy Gordon Delaney, well, he certainly could make things easy for her.

Whatever she might be planning!

CHAPTER 9

I spent Thursday morning Christmas shopping in Rabun County and had managed to check virtually everyone off my list, much to my surprise. I took what Andrea had said to heart and hit all the flea markets in the area, stopping in at my favorite one on the way back to Sweet Briar. It happened to be attached to the salvage yard where I'd had the misfortune of discovering Edith Plank's body under a pile of boards.

Yeah, I know.

Despite the unpleasant association, I still loved the place and stopped to get the last of the items I needed to make everyone a handmade art piece gift. It didn't hurt that Dolores, a blue tick hound, along with her adorable puppies, were in-house, and I needed a well-deserved break to get some cuddle time in. Rowdy Harpin, the establishment's owner, was only too happy to show them off once he finished fishing a candy bar out of his pocket and handing it over to me surreptitiously with a smile. A habit he started with Andrea when she was a little girl and never outgrew, and now passed on to me.

"Oh my...they have gotten so big!" I squealed, and I was overwhelmed by wriggling little bodies and tiny wet noses. "They are adorable!"

"Yeah. The pups are about five weeks old now and could go to their new owners by seven weeks, but I don't let any of my pups go to their new homes until they are ten or eleven weeks old. I give them time with their momma so she can teach them manners. Plus, you shouldn't ever bring a puppy into the picture around Christmas time. It's just too hectic, and there is so much going on that a little puppies' needs might not get met. You know?"

Wise words. I knew this was Rowdy's last litter of pups, and he was a conscientious breeder. I wished more were like him.

Before I left the salvage yard, I asked Rowdy if he had received any of the mystery notes. He told me he had and that he was coming with 'his missus' and couldn't wait to see what this was all about.

Back in my truck, I started my engine and tuned my radio to the eighties station, then turned up the dial as The Psychedelic Furs sang about a girl who was Pretty in Pink. The passenger seat was loaded to the gills with my finds that I would turn into unique items. Then my thoughts turned back to this case—if that's what you'd call it.

I no longer had my 'in' to the police department with Brian, so I couldn't mine him for information to help me with my snooping. I scolded myself for failing to take advantage of having him right in front of me last night, where I could have risked asking for information. I wanted to know if the police had tracked down who had hired the planes towing the banners. Our note-maker had to be the one to hire them. Solving this case might be as simple as having that answer.

Hey! Wait a minute! Nothing was stopping me from finding that out for myself. Total 'duh' moment there, Lily.

I hurriedly pulled over to the side of the road and perused my phone, searching for plane companies that you could hire for advertising, and even noted a few of them in North Carolina. Especially since I could pick up a rock throw it; confident, it would land in that state from several sites near our town. After a few minutes, I realized calling them could wait until I was back in the comfort of my office. Who knew there were so many plane companies around here?

Sighing, I tossed my phone back in my handbag, but not before noting Becky had tried to call me several times. That could wait until I arrived at my office as well. Pulling back on the road, I wondered if a few minutes of making phone calls would be the end of this mystery and give me the answers I was seeking. Could it be that easy?

I was distracted by my thoughts and didn't notice the sedan coming up quickly behind me until I heard the horn and caught the car in my rearview mirror. Then it crossed the doubled yellow lines illegally and flew past me. Adriana! She even gave me a little wave as she peeled away at top speed. The telltale sounds of Charlie Daniels warning about the Devil being down in Georgia followed in her wake. Even though my sites now turned to Nora as my main suspect, my granny was still acting awful suspicious, and I knew I couldn't rule her out just yet.

Sigh. Why couldn't I have normal relatives?

* * *

IT TOOK three trips to unload everything from my truck, and I was exhausted as I parked George in his prominent spot in the front of my shop. I had an enormous patch of gravel that had dead grass growing that I hadn't gotten around to pulling, and if I parked over that spot, it hid the weeds. I stood back and surveyed the view, noting that George would make a suitable advertising vessel. I could paint my shop's name on him and leave him parked here, only using him for junking trips. I was nervous about the thought of taking on car payments, but I didn't think I'd survive a summer down here without air conditioning. I'd just have to see what my finances could handle now that I'd be taking on a home renovation come spring.

As I was rushing back in the warehouse and up to my loft, Lorcan showed up and was close on my heels.

"Lorcan! I had this great idea to start calling all the airplane rental companies in the area!"

"Lily..."

"I found a bunch of listings for Georgia but thought I should also check out those in North Carolina because—yeah—so close!"

"Lily, listen..."

"I'm going to get right on it now, and I think I may have this enigmatic note leaving menace in my clutches. I can feel it."

"Lily! Will you hush and listen to me a minute?" Lorcan huffed out; his voice raised a bit in frustration.

"I....huh? What's wrong?" I asked, finally hearing him.

"Becky Nolan has been trying to reach you. It seems a large shipment has arrived at her shop, addressed to you. She wanted to know if you ordered anything and had it sent to her. Becky told me she wouldn't open the boxes in case you had done so, but she had to close early today, so she finally called here when she couldn't get you on the phone to leave the message. Becky said she'd be in bright and early tomorrow if you want to stop in after your lessons with Hortense and Hermione.

"What the *heck?* I didn't order anything, nor had it sent there. Did she give you any more information?"

"No. Just that she will be in early tomorrow, and you can either stop by before you start your lessons or right after to get them."

Well, that was just weird and alarming. I know I had nothing to do with boxes showing up at Becky's bookstore, so that means someone else sent them there and addressed them to me.

"What are you thinking, Lily?" Lorcan asked, his brow furrowed with concern.

"I'm apprehensive about these boxes...because I didn't send them to Becky's shop. That means someone sent them addressed to me, and when I open the boxes, they will go, 'Boom!' and I will spend Christmas in the hospital—or worse."

Lorcan didn't agree or disagree; he just acknowledged my worry with a great, big hug. I felt myself relax into his embrace and enjoyed the cedar and spice combo of his cologne tickling my nose when I heard someone clearing their throat behind us.

We jumped back like toddlers with their hands caught in the cookie jar.

Standing at the top of the stairs was my Aunt Iona, my mother's sister, and my Aunt Chiara, my father's sister. In between both was Lorcan's mother, Eileen, who had a slightly bemused look on her face. "Are we interrupting anything?" she asked.

"What? No! NO! We were just talking—and stuff." I ended lamely.

Lorcan was seven shades of red and rushed over to his mother, hugging her.

"Handing out a lot of these lately, aren't you, dear?" Eileen chuckled.

I peered at both my aunts inquisitively and asked them why they were here, then realized that sounded a bit rude, so I added how happy I was to see them both. My Aunt Chiara, one eyebrow raised, accepted my hugs, then pulled her gloves off and tucked them into her handbag before responding.

"The three of us just had a late lunch at the new Irish pub on Peach Lane off the square. Have you been yet? No? It's delightful without being contrived or cute. A nice place with great Shepherd's Pie and stellar beer on tap. Might make a nice place to go on a date." She stated a bit too pointedly for my comfort.

I cleared my throat and chuckled awkwardly. "Yeah, like I have time for that. So, you just stopped in to say hello?" I probed.

"Among other things," Aunt Iona spoke up, "We've been discussing Christmas Day dinner."

Groan. When I saw my two aunts standing there, I knew that the subject of where I would be spending my first Christmas, first holiday as it were, would come up. They figured I would be here and knew they could corner me and settle the issue once and for all. I just hoped they would shed no blood. Theirs or mine!

Aunt Chiara explained. "It's all been settled. Christmas Eve, everyone in this town will be busy on the square with whatever our note-writing trickster has planned for this fun little event. Come Christmas Day; we decided it would be sad for you to wake up all alone in your apartment, so after the events of the night before, you are to come home with your Uncle Stephen and me and spend the night with us— you can bunk up with Andrea since she has two double beds in her room." Aunt Chiara held her hand up as I was about to start arguing. "You will get to wake up and open presents with us. Adriana and Antonio have already agreed to spend the night in the guest room. Then we will all have a ridiculously huge breakfast where your uncle, joined by Steve Junior, will go all out, stuffing you silly with his French Toast and waffles, pastries. He may even get out the crepe pan and leave you in a state of cathartic bliss." She finished.

"After a very long walk to my home to digest that splendid repast," Aunt Iona picked up the conversation, "you will get to open even more presents and have Christmas dinner with your Uncle Owen and me." Aunt Iona stated. "Eileen and Henry are coming over with Lorcan...you are coming to our house, dear," she turned to Lorcan, informing him of this development, then continued. "Even Lorcan's grandfather, Malcolm, will be joining us, and I've asked June and Dennis over, along with Jake, for dessert, and we're watching It's A Wonderful Life and A Christmas Carol...so everything has been settled, and you need not fret." Aunt Iona smiled when she finished her proclamation. I walked over to my desk and sat.

Well then.

After that, the three ladies hurried out, leaving Lorcan and me in a daze, and Lorcan, at least, chuckling at how well our families managed to come up with a solution that would work for all.

"What just happened here?" I asked.

"That was hurricanes, Iona, Chiara, and Eileen all converging to make sure we'd be too overcome with their sheer will to dare argue any changes to their plans for our Christmas Day. It's a rather decent plan, and I'm glad I will get to have Christmas dinner with you, although I almost want to be with you at your Dolce family breakfast. Your Uncle Stephen's spread is going to give me visions of sugarplums and pastries from now until the big day."

"You could always come over and sleep with us." I paused, cringing when I heard what came out of my mouth. I quickly finished up with, "I guess it is a pretty good arrangement. Andrea is going to be thrilled when she hears about it. She has been begging me to have a sleepover with her since I arrived in town!" I smiled, then glanced inquisitively at Lorcan as he started to laugh out loud.

"That's the only bad thing about this entire scheme of theirs." He gave me a rueful look. "Andrea is famously reported to snore like a lumberjack. You better have a pair of earplugs or noise-canceling headphones, or you won't get one iota of sleep with her in the same room!"

Well great.

Lorcan and I decided to grab a late lunch of our own but at June's Emporium. Not because she sold her delightful treats to her customers, but because I accepted her invite and extended it to Lorcan when she informed me she'd made grilled cheese and minestrone. Most people would raise an eyebrow and ask just why we were both excited at the prospect of something rather mundane in its offerings. We'd just laugh knowingly amongst ourselves because it would be evident that someone had never had June's grilled cheese sandwich or her minestrone!

An in-depth description of said treat wouldn't do it justice. June used three different gourmet cheese on home-made thick white loaf bread. She buttered the bread with herbed butter she made herself from her Irish grandmother's recipe. Then while said sandwich was grilling, she sprinkled a fourth gourmet cheese, shredded on top of one side, flipped the concoction, and did the same on the other side, steaming it under a lid with a few sprits of water for a few seconds before flipping it once more and then plating it. The result was a cheesy crispy shell on the outside with insanely thick, perfectly toasted bread enveloping the most delectably melted cheese you've ever sunk your teeth in.

The minestrone? It was heavy on the tomato side, with

impeccably chopped vegetables, everything fire-roasted and slow-cooked to perfection. Ideal for dipping your sandwich in or just slurping down with abandon. Why June chose a general store with witchy and standard odds and ends when she could have a restaurant was beyond me. But I never turned down one of her grilled cheese lunches! Ever.

My mood had soured a tad when we reached the back door, and I found yet another note taped to it. As usual, this one was cryptic, but now it appeared some kind of demented game would be afoot—if the residents of this town decided to play, that is.

Lorcan studied the note over my shoulder as I read it aloud:

RAVEN LOOKS FOR CLUES IN THE PAGES OF HER BOOK.
GATHER THE ITEMS, BUT DON'T BE A CROOK!
ONLY THE VICTORS WILL CLAIM THE PRIZE.
BUT THE GREATEST OF ALL IS IN THE HANDS OF THE WISE!
(Seriously...take more than one, and your fingers will turn black! You've been warned!)

WHAT MANNER of evil was this? Was this some kind of crazy game, and how could we possibly understand these stupid rules? Wait a minute! Books! Becky Dolan said she'd received a shipment of boxes in my name. Could those be the items in question, if indeed there were books inside? I turned to Lorcan, who was now holding the door open to the shop's back entrance. June met us at the door, nodding her head in understanding.

"I received one as well. It was on my car windshield this time. And yes, I am just as unnerved as you, my dear. I didn't understand it at first, but then Becky Dolan called, saying she was searching for you. She was supposed to go up to Cherokee today to hang with her college friend, but her friend called, saying she came down with a cold. Becky is here instead, so come on in and have something to eat.

We walked into the kitchen, and I greeted Becky, who was indeed at the table. Excitement was written all over her face.

"Lily! Hi, Lorcan. Sit. I believe I have some of this figured out...these puzzles. I hope you don't mind, but I opened your boxes and found something I think you will find very interesting. But before we get to that, look at this."

Becky had the notes arranged on the table and jotted some things down in a notebook like she pieced the puzzle together to find an answer to these riddles.

We sat and began munching away on the divine grilled cheese sandwiches while June ladled soup into cups so we could sip or dip. I was contemplating what Becky had started to push towards me just as Andrea walked in.

"Oh, good! You are here. I got a text from Becky that we were brainstorming. What's with the boxes...and yes, please, June. But just a half sandwich. I've already eaten." Andrea sat, and we all looked at Becky to explain.

"Alright. The first riddle invites everyone who gets one to the town square on Christmas Eve. Pretty straightforward. Asks that we bring something to eat enough for a crowd. Again, nothing too unusual. The second letter then sets up a scenario where no one needs to worry about having gifts, that this is a place for friends and family. That got me thinking, and I started calling everyone I know and polled people as they came into my shop. Every single person who received a note has one thing in common." She sat back and gazed around the room expectantly.

"What is it?" June asked in alarm, raising her hand to her throat.

"They are either related to, friends with, are good acquaintances of our new resident dark witch, Lily Sweet. Everyone, to my knowledge, knows Lily in some way."

Lorcan finally appeared concerned enough to broach the obvious when he asked, "Are you sure? I mean, I know a lot of the same people Lily does and, oh, wait. I am not related to some. And, wow, are you sure?" He asked, rubbing his neck and cutting his eyes over to me.

"I'm sure," Becky stated. "Every person knows each other in some way. But Doreen and Donald? They aren't related. They are friends of a sort. You certainly know them well, Lorcan. But the Dolce's don't, except for Lily. Stu? When was the last time Stu got invited to an event with either the Dolce clan or Croys, for that matter? Specifically, the Croys married into the Haywood clan? I can't see Judge Owen and Stu having much in common, can you? Even though they often see each other because of what Stu does for the town. But the one thing that ties everyone invited together is Lily. They are all related, friends and acquaintances of our Lily here."

What did Stu do for the town, I wondered?

Andrea looked gobsmacked and pulled the paper with all the riddles written down on it to her side of the table to read them better.

"It says 'no gifts, but someone will get the prize.' What do you think that means?"

"That's where I start to get beyond confused." Becky maintained, running her hand through her flaxen mane and blowing out a frustrated sigh. "What is meant by that? If there are no gifts to be exchanged, what is meant by the word 'prize?' Obviously, dancing, singing, and Christmas carols will be aplenty...and even Santa might make an appearance. I was going over this with Jake this morning at breakfast; he warned it could mean we all had to finish partying by eleven so the religious among us could get to midnight services. And parents could put their kids to bed before midnight and Santa's believed arrival."

"You had breakfast with Jake?" Andrea asked, "When? Where? I didn't see you at the café."

Becky blushed, charmingly, and glanced down, then mumbled, "Oh...we happened to bump into each other at Joe's and shared a booth."

Lorcan, Andrea, and I all made eye contact and grinned. June made motions with her hands as if she was asking us to stop teasing poor Becky. So, we swallowed what would be our good-natured ribbing, and I cleared my throat, asking her a question to distract from the awkwardness.

"Right after that, we had the incident on the square with the planes. They hinted at a book. What did you figure out about the rest of it? Because it's not much." I argued.

"Well, it stated next time, buy the book. Buy, not B and Y, but to purchase one. Then today's note. Raven looks for clues, and again, book. So, I thought it must allege to my bookshop, The Reading Raven. That's what made me open your boxes, Lily, and I found this."

Becky pulled a tiny book out of one of the boxes near her feet and handed it to me. It was a simple tome, a pamphlet really, all paper with a plain cover with a sweet briar rose on it and nothing else. It was about four inches tall and three inches wide, or close enough in my estimation. The cover was a light reddish-brown. The rose was in black ink. Inside the pages were cream, and the edges all around were jagged.

Each page had some clues and an item to find with cryptic messages on how to go about finding them.

Andrea and Lorcan had pulled out their copies. Lorcan was the first to speak.

"It's a scavenger hunt!"

"No. It's more than that. Look!" cried Andrea. "What do these numbers mean?"

I examined the page where she was pointing, and everything suddenly clicked as far as what we beheld. "It's like that geocaching game some people do. You use coordinates to find the location with your phone and find a spot where something is hidden, take one item and then move on to the next location."

"Geo-what-zing?" June seemed perplexed, so I went to her computer and pulled up a Geocaching site so she could read up on the phenomenon. "Well, this seems like harmless fun then, no? I mean, it even asks that whoever plays the game only takes one item at each location. So. it might just be good honest fun."

"Yes, but this game comes with a warning," I stated. "If anyone takes more than one, someone will curse the thieves with black fingers. Therefore, we have just found one very crucial detail out." I proclaimed.

"What is it?" Andrea wrinkled her forehead and kept scrutinizing the booklet like it would start speaking and impart all its knowledge to her at any minute.

"Whoever is behind this is a witch. There is no way that person could know if someone would take more than one from each location and promise retribution of darkened fingers if some kind of spell wasn't put on each box hiding the prizes."

Lorcan rubbed his hand under his chin and nodded yes like he agreed with my theory, then looked up at me and smiled. "Now we just have two questions remaining. Who is behind these puzzles? And who is the wisest of all who will figure out that last line in the riddle? 'The greatest of all is in the hands of the wise.' What the heck does that mean? Will all the prizes combined lead you to a bigger one? The greatest one? And what is meant by 'hands of the wise' I wonder?"

You and me both, bucko, you, and me both.

CHAPTER 10

*W*ord spread quickly among the guests if you could call them that, and Becky was inundated with my family and friends, all wanting to purchase their copy of the little tome. Even those without invitations were getting their hands on it and getting into the act. I kept hearing about the locations of different sites around Sweet Briar where the hidden boxes with their tiny prizes were. It didn't escape my notice that no matter how many people claimed the items, there was always enough in the cache for the next person who came around. I suspected self-regenerating magic was afoot.

I was happy to find out that all the money collected in book sales was going to our local no-kill shelter. At least something good was coming out of this.

Someone found the first box the very next day. I heard about it while at my potion's lessons with the Winters. Gordy Polk was Becky's first customer and brought the booklet with him on his garbage run. He found the first item by—as he put it—deduction and a little luck. The first page showed a private server web address and instructed the reader to sign up for a 'hide and seek' account. The next page showed a tiny silver snowflake, a tree, and had coordinates written down. When Gordy put the coordinates in, he said it led him to a site, and he spent ten minutes looking around until he found the box with a small prize inside. He wouldn't tell us where it was and said that would just 'ruin all the fun for everyone else.'

Thankfully, tomorrow was Saturday, and everyone I knew would be running hither and yon searching for these prizes. Even Hermione and Hortense were getting antsy and wishing they could close the shop for the day and get a head start on everyone else.

"But you will get a head start on some of us," I maintained. "You are only open until two o'clock. You can go out this afternoon and have at it."

"Yes, Lily...but we are just upset some of the players have already been out there. It's not fair to us business owners. What if they get the grand prize before we do?"

I didn't think that was how this would work, but both sisters wouldn't listen to my reasoning. Therefore, it was a fretful hour of lessons, and I was glad to be done for the week when they were over. Hortense was so distracted, and she barely noticed I mixed the wrong potion giving me an A for effort anyway! I poured my concoction down the drain in case it wound up in some poor unsuspecting soul's morning tea in error!

Speaking of souls, Hester and Chester Soule—sounds like ghoul—the town undertakers had cornered me after my lesson. I was in front of the tea shop when I bumped into them, and they informed me how excited they were about the upcoming event. I was so shocked to find out they, too, had received the notes, I forgot to block my thoughts, and Hester zeroed in on them.

"No, dear. I don't think this has malicious intent behind it.

Not at all. If this were dark magic's, we'd all be fighting and quarreling amongst ourselves to beat our neighbors to the hidden boxes. Dark magic brings out the worst in people, and that isn't happening."

Her announcement didn't fool me or bring any relief to my worries. Especially since she was sporting a pair of running shoes, and Chester had a matching pair. That and the fact that they both were staring daggers at Hermione and Hortense, who were giving them equally matching scowls filled with venom from inside the tea shop.

What was going on here? A rivalry of some sort?

"No. Ahem...not a rivalry. We just intend to beat the pants off those two." Chester grunted out in his odd throaty voice.

Damn it. Get out of my head. Block! And the sisters only wore tight dresses and short skirts; they wouldn't be caught dead in pants.

"I could easily arrange that," tittered Hester menacingly.

Gah!

I barely had time to throw up a barrier spell to shield my thoughts when I saw Hermione rush to the front of the shop and throw open the door. Hortense was still inside, running around, turning lights off, and shutting down their many tea kettles. Before I knew what was happening, both sisters locked up their business tight, flipped the sign from 'Open' to "Closed," and ran to their car.

"Oh no, they don't! Hurry Brother! Get to our bike. They think they are going to win, but we know better now, don't we?"

With that, Hester and Chester ran to a parked motorcycle complete with a bullet-shaped sidecar, planted helmets on their heads, and hightailed it after the sisters, who were going way faster than our posted speed limit, which left me with one thought. If that wasn't proof that some kind of dark magic was behind this, especially after Hester's emphatic attitude to the contrary, I don't know what else it could be!

I spun around to head over to my truck and on to lessons with Tanaquil but stopped short when I found Officer Delaney standing behind me wearing a smirk.

"What do you want?" I asked as I moved to go around him.

Gordon reached out and grabbed my arm, then leaned down and spoke to me in a quiet voice. "You need to stop making trouble for me and ruining things if you know what's good for you."

"I don't know what you mean. I haven't done anything to you. Now move out of my way."

"Or what? You gonna call the cops?" The grimace on Gordon's face was chilling, and I would have felt more threatened had I not felt pretty confident in my abilities now that I had a few solid weeks of training under my belt and had upped my dark magic lessons the last three days. That and the fact that I spied both Sheriff Glen Buford and Brian walking towards us, not that I needed their aid. I could take Officer Delaney with one hand tied behind my back.

"Everything OK here?" Brian was quick to ask. Gordon blushed slightly and stepped away from crowding me the way he was.

"Sure," He sneered, turning away from the two men, and giving me an ugly look, "I was just telling Lily here to watch out for all her crazy relatives running wild around town searching for needles in haystacks. That dumb game could turn dangerous if something bad were to happen to one of them, what with the road conditions getting worse in this cold weather." He smiled coldly at the Sheriff, and Brian then turned and walked back toward the police station.

Glen lowered his head and sighed, "I am not sure why he took such a dislike to you, Lily. He's a good deputy, but unless he can curb that attitude, I may have to request he put in a transfer."

I held my tongue because, let's face it; I'd love it if I saw the back end of Deputy Delaney driving out of town forever.

I risked a scolding for being too nosy yet asked both men if they had tracked down the pilots of those two advertisement planes. Both men gave me puzzled looks.

"Why would we do that, Lily?" Brian asked me.

"Because of your case. I figured the easiest way of finding out who the culprit is would be to call around and find out who hired them. This way, you'd be closer to solving it. And with the books showing up addressed to me at Becky's shop, I figured you could track where it originated, no?" I added lamely, unsure of myself when I noted their confusion deepen, and a glance passed between them.

"Lily. I'm not sure what has you so spooked, but there is no case. We aren't investigating the origin of these notes. Why would we?" Sheriff Glen asked. "A body hasn't turned up, has it?"

"No, a body hasn't turned up! But the fireworks were malicious. What if someone had a heart attack thinking there was a shooting at the school? What if..."

"Whoa! Lily. Slow down. The Kowalski boys were charged with a misdemeanor and paid a fifty-dollar fine apiece. We can't prove they found a note daring them to shoot off those firecrackers because if there was such a note, it burned up when the explosions started. It's only their word that ever tied it to these other ones showing up around town. There isn't any crime, so why look into anything?" Brian stated.

"It's bizarre. Sinister even. Don't you think?"

"The entire thing is eccentric but not evil, Lily. I don't know why you are jumping to conclusions?" Sheriff Glen sighed with exasperation. I could tell he was losing patience with me.

"Because...because this entire puzzle focuses on people who I am either related to or are my friends. It points back to me. Becky Dolan discovered this clue and it has me freaked out to tell you the truth. Everyone I know and love will be in the town square in nine days. What if it's a planned maneuver by an enemy of my family? And has something to do with what happened in the past? What if they are all injured by some witch attack—or worse?" I felt myself losing a bit of sanity and began breathing rapidly. I couldn't embrace the notion that this was a bit of fun because so much had happened recently in my world that equaled danger that I had no control over. Could anyone blame me for being shellshocked?

"Lily. I promise I won't let anything bad happen to you or anyone at this—whatever it is—on Christmas Eve. The entire police department is on call, the county as well. We take shifts on Christmas Day, but we will be out and about and keep an eye on the square that night. With the fact that powerful witches will fill the village green, someone would be crazy to attack with that much magic floating around. It doesn't work that way. Trust me, OK?" Brian broke with protocol, ignoring the distance building up between us, and pulled me into an embrace. I allowed him to do so because, quite frankly, it felt good having someone envelop me in their arms. At that moment, I needed a hug.

There. I admitted it. Lily Sweet. The girl who shied away from human contact and lived like a hermit crab since forever needed a hug. *Pardon me.*

As Glen and Brian departed, they both gave me more assurances that they'd be out and about on Christmas Eve, and I had nothing to worry about as long as they were in charge of things. Alrighty, then.

I didn't have much else planned for my day and decided to head back to my apartment. I rounded the corner in front of June's Emporium along the building's side, which led to the rear deck and entrance. I paused when a movement to my left caught my eye. Wicked came sauntering around the fence along the back of June's property and trotted up the steps, pausing to wait for me to catch up and open the door to let her inside.

"What are you doing out here? How did you get outside, Missy? You are not supposed to be running around the neighborhood!" I scolded. Wicked just ignored me. When I reached her, she lowered her head and dropped something at my foot that she'd been holding in her mouth.

"What is that?"

I reached down and picked up a tiny plastic snowflake. Is that? It couldn't be, could it?

"Did you go geocaching for this? But, but how could you, though? You are a cat! It appears to be the first item in the booklet. Cats can't go geocaching! They can't!"

Wicked gave me a little, "Mreow," and looked smug.

"There is no way I am going to believe you found the first hiding spot, opened the box, and pulled out this tiny snowflake. There is no way!"

Wicked stared at me a minute. Then I'd swear she did a cat version of an eye roll, jumped up on the door, managing to get the knob to turn so it would open, and squeezed through into the foyer. I meekly followed. Once in, she trotted into the kitchen where June, who I could already hear making happy exclamations to my talented feline, immediately got out some kibble to feed her.

Sigh. Why can't I have a normal cat?

* * *

THE WEEKEND BECAME an insane relay race of sorts. It seemed each of my friends and relatives had gone loco and tried to outdo the other to become the first to find all the locations and tiny 'prizes' listed in the book. I'd searched through it several times and could find no hidden meanings or evil undertones. It just seemed like a fun and distracting game. I still couldn't shake the fear, and my reticence to embrace the merriment had a lot to do with being confronted by Deputy Delaney. He warned me to stop making trouble for him— and by that, I figured he meant my cousin, Nora, as well. But I hadn't done anything and wondered if it pointed to her as the note-maker. But I couldn't focus on that right now because I was dealing with insanity all around me.

Not that I wanted to, but all I had to do to immerse myself in the craziness was walk around the square. I was heading to Joe's Diner when the first bit of lunacy started in the form of Gloria Stillwell...one of the Witch Elders and the last person I would suspect would get caught up in this scavenger hunt.

"Did you see her?" Gloria all but screeched at me as I walked toward her car. She parked at the curb in front of Joe's.

"Um...who?"

"Sophia. Your cousin. Did you see her drive past? Which way did she head? I bet she went left down Main towards your place. I knew she'd try to trick me."

"Uh...no. I didn't see anyone drive by. Is everything..."

"Well, I can't stop and chit-chat—I need to get to the next hidden box."

And with that, she jumped in her Mercedes and tore off down Main Street after my cousin. I think. I watched Gloria's car and didn't notice Susanne Washington walking up the sidewalk behind me until she called out, jolting me out of my reverie.

"Lily! Lily, come here. Is this a three or an eight? My eyesight isn't what it used to be."

"Hello, Susanne. How is choir practice going?"

"No time for that, dear. What is this number? I just saw Gloria head left out of town, but I think someone tricked her into believing the next location is south of here. She doesn't have GPS in that fancy car of hers because it's an older model. Nor does she use a cell phone. So, I have the advantage, having both!"

"It's a three." I barely got that out of my mouth when Susanne, a typically reserved and proper older woman, thanked me and tore off across the street to her Buick sedan and flew out of town heading west. Whoa.

I reached the diner and went in and found utter chaos waiting for me.

"I did not cheat—you did. In all my years, I've never cheated at anything."

"You did so, Shirley. Gordy saw you push Doreen Murphy out of the way and grab that Christmas ornament from the box, then take off in your ambulance! Wait until the mayor finds out you are using government property on private time!" Sheila Polk screeched at her sister, our local EMT, then spun around and yelled at Joe in the doorway to his kitchen. "I'm leaving early. Everyone is getting those prizes, and I'm stuck here having to wait until we close. It's dead as a doornail, and Cindy can handle it." Cindy being the college-aged waitress filling the napkin-holders and smiling at the hysterics on display.

"Go ahead now, Sheila. Just calm down before your blood pressure goes wacky."

"Calm down! Calm down? How can I remain calm when my sister is cheating and made Stu cry? And wait until he hears the rest of what she's doing! He's going to be beyond upset! Now, I ask you, is that fair?" Turning back to Shirley, she cried, "You should be ashamed of yourself."

With that pronouncement, Sheila grabbed her handbag from behind the counter. Then she trotted past me with barely a nod as she swept through the door and out to her car. A moment later, she too tore off, heading west out of town. What did Shirley do to her brother to make him cry and bring down the wrath of Sheila?

"Hey, Shirley. What the heck is going on? Please tell me this silly game..."

"No time to talk, Lily!" I've got places to be and items to find!" And with that, Shirley charged past me, following the path her sister had just taken. In the ambulance, to boot!

"Joe. Please tell me I just imagined what happened here."

Joe came out of the kitchen with a mug and a carafe of coffee. Sighing loudly, he plunked it down on the table at my booth. He sat across from me and smiled.

"You didn't. Everyone has been going a little crazy this weekend with that scavenger hunt."

"But not you?" I asked, grinning as he pulled a pad and pen out of his pocket to write down my breakfast choice. I figured he would bus the tables too. Maybe the college kid couldn't handle multi-tasking as she was still stuffing napkins. "Two eggs, over medium, bacon, hash browns, grits on the side, and orange juice, please."

"Not me. I'm not interested in the scavenger hunt. It's not about that anyway."

"What do you mean?" I asked.

"Lily. Whoever is behind this is having a bit of fun with some of the residents in this town. I'm not going to get all caught up in the why and how. I will show up on Christmas Eve and enjoy the gathering of friends. That's what matters the most."

"So, do you think, um, that there is anything sinister

behind all this hoopla?" I trusted Joe's opinion and knew he'd impart a sound judgment on this confounding enigma.

"No. Relax, Lily. I know why you are asking. I also know you've been through a lot since you've arrived in town. Try to relax and enjoy this distraction. That's all it is." With that, Joe got up and made me my breakfast order. I'd like to say I could heed his advice and enjoy the days before the big holiday weekend coming up in a week, but I couldn't bring myself to do so. Not yet.

After downing my breakfast, I wandered back onto the street, hoping the lunacy would have decreased. It had not. I walked towards Fox Den Herbals and The Mystic Fox, two stores owned by Rita Chase, Brian's mother. Her assistant and master herbalist, Samantha Fairburn, stood outside watching the commotion going on over at The Reading Raven Bookstore, Becky's place.

"Hey, Samantha. What on earth is going on over there?" I asked, watching as two people I found vaguely familiar were standing in front of the shop screaming at my friend and making fools of themselves with all their arm flapping and foot-stomping. "Should we go save Becky?"

"Nah... she has it under control. From what I'm gathering, those two characters insisted they deserved one of those little booklets that showed up addressed to you because they are relations of some kind."

Now that I had a better vantage point, I realized it was Toby and Laura, no. Ted, and Linda. Wait! Todd and Lynn! That was it. Two very distantly related cousins I had only briefly met and didn't even live close. How did they even find out about this, and why were they here? I think they said the briefest of hellos to me, then smirked and left. It wasn't like we were close or would ever be close. Did they think this hunt meant an actual treasure?

"Maybe someone needs to tell them there isn't a prize

involved that I could tell. Unreal. Did you and Rita receive notes?"

"No. I'm not upset, though. Don't look that way, Lily. If I had to guess, one of your relatives is behind this. It must be because the puzzles are closely related to you and close friends. We are friends, I hope, but this seems different in some way. Maybe the falling out with Brian has something to do with why we aren't involved. That means someone close to you who is aware of the situation."

Yeah, and it made me nervous. In light of Deputy Delaney's comments, it could mean Nora was plotting something horrid. I hadn't seen a hair off her platinum head since I found she was back in town. Or it could be Adriana, pretending ignorance and up to some mischief. I just hoped it wasn't an unknown who wanted to cause me and those I loved some sort of unfortunate happenstance. We stood there a bit longer watching as Becky masterfully turned away the crazed ex-hippie cousins, then proudly stomp back to her shop and closed the door. I was just glad the beautician contingent hadn't come out to add their weight—and it was substantial—to the fight. Wise of them not to in light of how close they were to Cousin Nora. Hmm. Did that mean she was, indeed, behind all this?

I said my goodbyes to Samantha and thought the last of the weirdness was behind me. That was until I noticed Eileen and Henry read tailing my Aunt Iona. There was no other word for it. They were tracking her movements across the village green as she was staring at her phone. Aunt Iona wasn't paying much attention to her surroundings and almost walked straight into oncoming traffic. Which, in our sleepy town, wasn't necessarily a life-threatening event. She continued her way across the street, stopping in the alley between Carter's Hardware and June's Emporium, Dennis, and June Carter's respective shops.

That's when she let out a "Whoop!" and took off running up the alley. Eileen and Henry stopped short their stealthy pursuit, glanced at each other in alarm, then dashed after my aunt in what I could only describe as intense desperation. Who I didn't notice watching them was Jake, also on the hunt, it seems, until he slipped out of his hiding spot near the pharmacy and streaked up the alley behind Lorcan's parents and my aunt. Jake? OK, then. I assumed the geocaching was affecting them all. I could not believe this turn of events. Who knew everyone I loved in this town was insane?

Sigh. Why couldn't I have normal friends and relatives?

I sat down hard on one of the park benches, ruminating over all these strange happenings that I just witnessed. I decided tonight I would stake out the town and see if the mysterious note-writer would leave one more before the Christmas weekend was upon us. I couldn't see I had much choice because I didn't have any other ideas on what to do. I'd just finished accepting my decision and was readying myself to stand when Wicked chose that moment to jump up on the bench and sit next to me, dropping another item from her mouth.

It was a tiny red Christmas ball ornament. I wouldn't need to join in on the fun at this rate, not when my wicked feline could manage it for me.

CHAPTER 11

I was dressed entirely in black and had a mild shadow cloaking spell cast on me by Cousin Andrea, ironic since my instructors recently deemed me a Shadow Dancer. However, tracking dark magic and becoming invisible were two different forms of magic. At least I assumed they were. With nothing more to do the rest of Sunday, I had gone home to my apartment, laid out some dark clothing, caught up on my witchy studies and read the afternoon away, made a can of soup, fed Wicked, who seemed upset that I dragged her home with me, and went to bed by five that night. I dropped like a stone.

When my alarm went off at the stroke of twelve, I felt rested and ready for some midnight recognizance and planned on catching the perpetrator of mischievous note-making red-handed. Especially in light of how cold I found the early morning air. We had reached a low of twenty-eight degrees, which left me shivering, confident my nose looked like Rudolph's. Santa should be here any minute now to ask me to lead his team of reindeer. I didn't realize Georgia could reach such temperatures, and I was grateful I had on a warm pair of gloves.

I felt guilty about leaving Lorcan out of my plans, but as Andrea was standing guard, or rather, dozing in a frozen heap in her car positioned across the village square from my hiding spot, I knew I wasn't alone and had backup. Lorcan would be upset, but I felt guilty for all the lost sleep I had already caused him.

Nothing moved. The only action in the last hour had been Officer Delaney's squad car making a lazy loop around the square before he came to a stop outside the police station and went inside. I guessed he was on night duty. If that was the case, it meant he usually slept days and would explain why I hadn't seen Nora around town. She was probably with him and keeping similar hours. I tracked him from his patrol car to the front door, and if looks could kill, he'd be a pile of ash on the steps.

The last hour things had been quiet.

With just the soft glow from the Christmas lights illuminating the square and many shops, the village green seemed particularly enchanting. The various trees, entirely covered in twinkling lights, added to the festive charm. On the first weekend in December, the Christmas Festival had the town coming alive with tourists. I was still amazed at how many of them adored our magical theme and came especially for our more witchy offerings. That was the last big tourist weekend until early spring kicked off the next season, and our town was now ours to enjoy.

I was excited at the prospect of my shop's success, knowing my artistic creations were whimsical and usually garnered exclamations of joy at how magical they appeared. Who knew all along I was making sculpture and crafts that were heavy on the witchy charm. But it was in my blood, so I guessed I shouldn't have been so shocked. I'd made some solid sales that weekend and suspected I'd made the right decision to open my shop, Found Things. I was excited about the new year and all it would bring.

I was so distracted by my thoughts that I almost missed the movement on the corner of Main Street. Jerking upright, I watched a slight figure dressed all in black, moving stealthily along the sidewalk near the diner. Waiting like an owl perched on a branch high above while the mouse made its way to the targeted place of attack, I knew I had my prey sighted, especially when I saw the mysterious figure pull a note out of their pocket and tape it to the diner door.

It was time to make my move. I sent Andrea a text to ready herself should the figure take off running in her direction and prayed the incoming text would make enough noise to awaken her in time.

What happened next would go down in this village's lore and be repeated in stories for generations to come.

* * *

"WHAT WERE YOU THINKING? Are you that insane that you'd risk burning down this town to spite your great-grandmother?"

"I am not the only one at fault here. Adriana started this! She lobbed some kind of dark, evil something—bad—at my head. I still don't know what she did. Look at me! I look like a chimney cleaner!" I was covered from head to foot in soot. I didn't appreciate Brian yelling at me so early in the morning...or any time for that matter.

"You started it. Not me." That was Adriana acting all huffy from her seat inside Brian's police vehicle.

"You tried to kill me!"

"You threw fire at me. What was I supposed to do? Duck?"

"You sent those bat things at my head...they exploded! You

threw exploding bats at my head, and now I look like I reside in a fireplace! Look at this soot!"

"You tackled your poor, old granny to the ground. You could have injured me—or worse!"

"You rolled over and drop-kicked me across the street. Old my a..."

"Ladies! Stop this now!" Brian yelled even louder, and the crowd that had gathered gasped at his vehemence.

Oh yeah. The crowd. Um, you see, Adriana and I had managed to awaken the entire town, it seems. The reason they were all awake probably had something to do with the fire department. And the volunteer fire department. All the available police. Even the citizen watch arrived.

Why?

We might have possibly gotten a tad too enthusiastic in our sparring if the village square's charred remains, the burned-out gazebo, and the blackened-singed trees were to be considered evidence. I couldn't identify my target fast enough before Adriana had gone on the defensive. She didn't recognize what was attacking her because Andrea slept through the entire melee until the fire trucks showed up, horns blaring and lights flashing. So, I remained cloaked.

We had managed to destroy the entire village square and scorch a few buildings before all was said and done.

It was unfortunate, but the transformers blowing behind us did have a certain pyrotechnic extravaganza charm that had Stu giving me yet another thumbs up when he'd arrived. Yeah, he definitely was into that stuff. The electric company vans getting ready to turn the power back on, adding to the commotion, couldn't erase the look of wonder on Stu's face.

"At least we now know who is behind these notes. I suspected grandmother, but I can't believe you'd do something so stupid."

"Shows how much you know. I'm not behind the notes."

She emphatically stated, then stuck her tongue out at me. Oh, that's mature.

"I caught you tacking one up on Joe's door! I have it in my hand, although it's a bit messy now, what with you tossing exploding bats my way!" I screamed.

"They aren't real bats, you ninny. Don't get all P.E.T.A. on me, for heaven's sake!" Adriana yelled back.

"Ladies!" Enough!" Brian again harangued and acting as if he'd rather be anyplace but here.

"We need to sort this out and put out all the fires, literally and figuratively, and now is not the time to continue arguing like this. What will the mayor think?"

The mayor? Is he here? Just who is the mayor anyway?

"I don't see any mayor. And we need to search my demon spawn granny for the rest of the notes. She's guilty."

"Guilty? Pulease! Here, Brian. Take them. You will see I am not the note-writer. Look at what I was trying to do."

Brian reached out and snatched the stack of papers Adriana held out, but not before I could nab a fresh one for myself. I read it over and over, and it indeed appeared similar to the notes the town's residents had been receiving the last few weeks but a poor substitute for one. Granny had tried, I'll give her that, but she must have used her old typewriter and a Reader's Digest because her notes didn't have the same pizazz as the originals. And her gluing skills left a lot to be desired. Along with her message:

PARTY IS CANCELLED. STAY HOME.
CHRISTMAS EVE IS FOR FAMILY, AND NO ONE IS
COMING.
STOP RUNNING AROUND TOWN LOOKING
FOR TOYS
SANTA ISN'T HAPPY, GIRLS AND BOYS!

(Stay home...the party isn't going on as planned...thanks for your interest...show up and you go on Santa's naughty list... you've been warned!)

"Um, I don't think she's our note-maker," I stated.

"You *think?*" This from Andrea, now fully awake and huddled on the bench behind me. She'd been crying and acted like a guilt-ridden wreck.

"Told you." Adriana sniffed, looking as insulted as a havoc-causing witch could muster when admittedly half of the destruction wrought had been by her hand.

"Why were you passing these out then?" I asked, the frustration in my voice evident.

"I wanted to stop this stupid event from happening, OK? Everyone you know in this town's invited, well, most. And the majority of your relatives too. But not me. Me!" Adriana tried to appear angry, but I, at least, could see the hurt in her eyes and realized she was so upset at being left out that she tried to have everyone believe someone canceled the party.

"Did you not realize everyone was off on the second phase of this prank? Every citizen has been chasing each other all over town, trying to find these hidden trinkets left in boxes at the location you can only find if you have the tiny booklet that came to Becky's shop. I don't think they would have believed this note." I argued.

"There won't be a party." Andrea lamented. "I mean, look at the square! It's ruined!"

She wasn't joking.

"Let's get you, ladies, some medical attention, and let the first responders get these fires out and the mess cleaned up. Things will seem better in the morning. I hope." Brian sighed, pulling out his phone and punching in numbers.

"Glen? Yeah. I have them. They are fine." He gave us a glance that said we were anything but fine. "Yes, tell Judge Owen and Cornelius to calm the Council down. No, I, yes. But, fine! Everyone else is here, being bystanders and gawking, Glen. I will get the patrols dispersing the crowd and sending everyone home once I talk to the mayor. Yes. Yes, he's here."

"You bet I'm here!"

Turning to see who spoke, I almost fell over when my eyes landed on our mayor.

"Stu? You're the mayor of Sweet Briar?"

Why didn't that surprise me? Stu Jones, the mayor of Sweet Briar, Georgia.

Sigh.

Why can't I live in a normal town?

CHAPTER 12

"*I* guess we can have a quiet Christmas Eve in front of the fire now." Aunt Iona surmised. "I mean, the square looks like a war zone, and there is no way we can clean it up before the event anyway. The Council refuses to let us use magic to make things right. Stubborn fools. This grumbling is coming from the Langsford-Planks and the Dietrich clan. Mark my words."

"It came from more than just they, my dear." Uncle Owen sympathized. "Several of the old families thought such an expenditure of magic without a vote would be too much to deal with before the holiday. They suggested we wait until the week between Christmas and New Year. I'm sorry, but the event seems like it won't be possible now."

"And we got all the hidden items too." Cousin Douglas grumped. I was surprised he had gotten in on the act as well, seeing as he usually kept to himself doing his own thing. Whatever that was. Doug was an enigma unto himself. However, he did have the telltale signs of a cheater since the tips of one hand had blackened. It looks like Dougie didn't heed the 'take only one—or else' that the puzzle had warned.

Even that didn't dissuade him. "Maybe we could try getting it a bit cleaned up. It's only Tuesday. Christmas Eve is Sunday."

"It's not going to happen, son. We have to resign ourselves to the fact that whatever bit of fun we were going to experience at this event is now, most certainly, canceled."

I felt like a weasel and shrunk in my chair, not speaking at all. I mean, what excuse could I offer for my behavior? I knew something horrific was going to happen. I just didn't realize I was that something terrible. Me, and Adriana, that is. I finished my dinner in silence with a few pitying glances coming at me from my family. Nothing I could say would alter the fact that Adriana and I made a monumental mess of things. I just needed to keep a low profile and hope for the best. I wondered what the person behind all this thought.

By Friday, I still couldn't shake my doldrums and found myself back at A Tale of Two Witches for my morning potions lessons.

"Here, Lily. Here is a list of all the potions I want to see you mix this morning. You have twenty minutes to mix all ten." Hermione stated. Great. Nothing like a morning slaving away at ten potions to pull a witch out of a slump. "When you finish, I will check them, and then you can bring the results to Adriana at your lessons today."

I got to work on my list, going over to my makeshift station and adding ingredients into my tiny cauldron. I was getting rather proficient at knowing the nuances of mixing ingredients and adding a pinch of this and a tad of that, giving my personal touch to the ones I had the liberty of embellishing. I also followed, with the strictest discipline, those that couldn't be one drop off. The result? After nineteen minutes and three seconds, I handed over all ten little bottles to Hermione and Hortense, who began to inspect my work.

"Oh my!" Hortense exclaimed. "Lily, you have outdone

yourself. These are perfect!" She did a little happy dance then reached under the counter to get a cardboard box with spaces to hold all ten bottles separate from one another. "Here, take this with you and make sure to tell Adriana you have surpassed our expectations." Blinking at both sisters, I thanked them and went on to my lesson with Tanaquil Alessi.

"Good morning, Lily. How are you, dear?" Tanaquil looked festive, dressed in emerald green velvet with a delicate strand of pearls around her swan-like neck. We have much to do today, so let's get right to it...shall we?"

I spent the next two hours dodging and casting one dark spell after another.

"Now...I am going to hit you with a series of four spells. That is all the information I am going to give you. I want you to sense them and try to block and or disable me. I have put up an absorption layer that will stop your spells from reaching me and causing me harm. The barrier only works going one way. Whatever I throw at you can and will wound you, however."

How nice.

I stood and waited for her next move. But to my surprise, Tanaquil walked over to her desk and sat, opened her book, and began to read. One minute went by—then two. Suddenly I felt before I heard the telltale signal that dark magic was heading at me. My brain rapid-fired thoughts of all I had learned in the last few weeks, and just before Tanaquil's magic slammed into me. I managed to cast out a repel spell and reversed her attack, watching it fizzle out when it hit her ward.

"That was lovely, dear."

Before she finished speaking, the next attack came, and I all but anticipated it, not letting her mild discourse distract me from trying to sense what was coming. This one came from above and was a binding spell that would have rendered me motionless. I sent my magic into it and caused it to dissolve before it made it halfway across the room.

The third spell came whirling behind me, and for a split second, I felt dizziness wash over me. I knew Tanaquil used very dark magic on me, but I couldn't figure out what it was. I started to panic, and then I realized Tanaquil was using my fear to feed her magic at the last second. I began to think pleasant thoughts, and instantly her magic weakened. That's when I discovered it was not a real threat but something to trick and confuse. I quickly knocked it back at the ward, where it popped out of existence.

I waited for the next and last one. Nothing. I could hear the clock ticking and watched Tanaquil reading leisurely at her desk, each page turn causing me to wonder when the attack would come. I felt sweat trickling down my brow and dared not wipe it away. I dared not move lest I miss any sign of her strike.

Suddenly, I heard a metal on metal sound but could not see the source. Looking back and forth, I sensed imminent danger but could not discover from where it was coming. The room had four doors, and all were open. The hallways beyond were dark, but I finally sensed movement and something like a glimmer of light hitting metal from the one to my north. Oh, my word!

Before I could scream in distress, I saw at least fifteen knives coming at me in midair of their own accord. How could? What the? How should I...argh! Inner flame, inner flame, inner flame! With no time to think or worry about the consequences, I forced myself to trust every instinct I had and opened myself to the darkest magic I possessed from the pit of my stomach. I knew my eyes had turned black, and I felt the darkness coiling up and out of me before I saw it come out of my fingertips. Some part of my brain realized this was all happening in seconds, but it felt like a slow-motion movie clip.

I raised my hands and let out a banshee scream sending everything I had at those knives, then squeezed my eyes shut from the force of magic that surged around me.

Then, utter silence.

I waited a moment before opening one eye, then the next. What I found left me dumbfounded. All fifteen knives had broken through Tanaquil's wards and were frozen in midair inches from her face and torso, quivering and pulsing with power. My power. As if awaiting my command. I realized my hands were still in front of me, trembling with magic. I concentrated on keeping them from moving forward and carefully made the motion to lower them gently on top of her desk.

Tanaquil remained composed. However, she was the palest I'd ever seen her. That was saying a lot, considering how snowy white her skin was in the first place. She didn't speak, yet she nonetheless raised her eyes to mine, and what I saw was relief and approval, and something else...respect.

"Excellent, Lily. Just excellent. Please take this letter with you and give it to Adriana. I must go compose myself, and I think a bit of tea to calm myself down after that display of power is in order, no?" Tanaquil showed me out, and I moved on to my last lesson of the week, back at my apartment with my great-grandmother.

"Hey, kiddo. What's all this?" Adriana greeted me, slightly subdued after last night. The two of us had been at odds with each other and had an uncomfortable week of lessons in light of our village destruction campaign of sorts.

"Hermione and Hortense wanted me to give you these potions I worked on this morning...and Tanaquil has this letter for you. I'm not sure why they wanted you to have them," I stated. Walking over to my recliner, I flung myself down and dropped my head in my hands.

"You look exhausted. What gives, cara?"

"What gives? We just destroyed the village green. Today I made ten potions. Five of which could kill a person in three seconds flat, leaving no trace for an unsuspecting officer, or rather, medical examiner not of the witchy variety to be able to detect—allowing me to get away with murder. Then I had a few hours of dodging spell attacks, with the last four tests of everything I have learned to date. The result? I sent a pack of knives flying at Tanaquil and almost impaled her where she sat, busting through her wards as if they didn't exist. She would have looked like a victim in a slasher movie had I not had the power to control the knives and drop them. That's what gives. I can't believe just four months ago I had no idea witches existed, now here I am doing dark magic and blowing up towns."

"Town. We haven't branched out yet, kid."

"You jest." I sniffed.

"I do. Liliana, why are you so glum?" Adriana came over to me and sat down on the loveseat, patting my knee.

"Don't you understand what today is?" I peered over at my granny and shook my head no. "Today is graduation day. You've done it, Liliana. You've mastered not only the basics, but according to Tanaquil's letter, you can control your darkest magic and surpassed everything she thought you could handle. You are a witch to be reckoned with, my dear!"

I sat back and began to chuckle. The chuckle turned into a laugh that caught in my throat, and I began to cry. All the stress of the last few weeks came to a head and left me a wretched mess. In a move so totally unexpected that it made my sobs dissolve in an instant, Adriana stood up, leaned over me, and gave me a hug and a kiss on the top of my head.

"There, there. You poor dear. Liliana, you've had a rough

few days. But sweetie, you are finished with your basic training. You are a witch! Anything you learn from this point forward will be advanced and focused on where your talents lie. You will have choices. You can decide how and when you want to pursue them. The Council will be satisfied with these reports, and your talents will go on record. From now on, you can rest assured you will have the respect and honor you are due."

"I don't understand. How? Why? What did I do that I'm suddenly OK?"

"What did you do? What did you do?! You just did five years of basic witch training in twenty-two days! There isn't a witch, alive or dead, who has done this, has the raw talent such as you. Liliana, don't you understand yet? You are the strongest dark witch to ever live in my memory, even stronger than I am. Although just try and get me to admit that to anyone else, ever." I laughed as Adriana harumphed and postured yet wondered at her words. Did I seriously complete all I needed to know, the basics anyway? And that quickly?

"But I still make mistakes!"

"Big deal. Just because you toss an errant spell or two here and there and burn down a village doesn't mean you aren't a powerful witch. It just means you need to settle down a bit more and focus or have something to keep you focused. Like a home renovation project or art studio." Adriana gave me a meaningful smile and a little wink. In that instant, I realized everything would be OK in my world. My confidence, while still lacking, was growing. The realization that four months ago, I could barely take care of myself in the 'real world,' and now I could defend those I loved with a few bumps and bruises along the way brought a sense of calm. I accepted this new reality.

* * *

CHRISTMAS EVE ARRIVED, and while no one was mentioning their intent for the day, most people I knew were keeping to themselves and not doing much at all. I didn't have much to do either and found myself curled up on my window seat, my plans for Christmas set. No further instructions had shown up. No notes. No messages in the sky. Nothing. I wondered what everyone would be doing this evening and picked up my phone to call Andrea. No answer.

The sky was overcast, and the temperatures had bottomed out in the upper thirties. Grabbing a sweater jacket, I wrapped myself up, added a matching knit cap and scarf, and then put on my suede boots. I wandered down to the empty Emporium. Wicked was nowhere in sight, and I suspected she'd gotten out again. If she were an average cat, I would have been frantic, but my cat? Yeah...I worried about the townsfolk with her on the loose, not the other way around. I grabbed my bag and noted how much heavier it felt. Peering inside, I was surprised to see a mass of mini items, all of them the tiny prizes from the hunt, and wondered who or what put them there. It more than likely was Wicked. That cat was beyond normal, and I finally admitted she was one magical fur ball.

Noting the time, I realized it was going on four-thirty and knew darkness would be descending shortly. I planned to stay in and have leftover minestrone, but suddenly I no longer wanted to be alone. I slung my bag over my shoulder and headed out to my truck.

Before I could reach George, I noticed movement out on the street. Turning in that direction, I walked around to the front of the Emporium and saw Lorcan walking towards me. Grinning and waving, I crossed the street and met him in front of the diner. He was layered to protect from the chill, wearing a heavy plaid jacket and had a scarf on as well. However, his head was bare, and he had a tousled look that suited him, his rich brown hair framing his face.

"Hey, stranger. Fancy meeting you here. I was just going to drive around town and mope. I didn't feel like being alone tonight, but I also don't feel like being among friends and family because I still feel miserable about what Adriana and I did." I lamented.

Lorcan wrapped me up in a big, warm bear hug. "First of all, Merry Christmas Eve. Second of all, putting yourself in a self-imposed exile is not the way to kick off the holiday weekend. It would be best if you were with friends. It's your first official holiday with us, and look. See? No hospital visits." Lorcan laughed a bit at the shock on my face as realization dawned that I was, in fact, standing upright and not languishing in a hospital room.

"That's right! I'm...wow. I guess I made it." I stated.

We slowly walked around the square, and I asked Lorcan what his plans were for the evening.

"I don't have any."

I smiled, then my face fell. "I guess I could go back to my apartment and have the soup I planned on having for dinner tonight. I was going to drive around and see if anyone else was doing out, but it seems everyone is in for the night and..." That's not right. No, upon further notice, Lorcan and I spied a few people walking from every direction around the town in small groups, all heading to the village square. What the...?

"What are they doing? That's, that's Aunt Iona and Uncle Owen, and Doug. Aunt Chiara as well." Turning to my left, I noticed June, Dennis, and Jake heading our way. Uncle Stephen, Andrea, and Steve Junior behind them with matching smiles on their faces. Across from us on our right, the Winters Sisters and Becky Dolan, with Martha Mosely just behind them, came into view. Everyone was carrying covered dishes, excited to be heading to the village green. "There's your mom and dad as well...and is that? That's your grandfather Malcolm. I've yet to meet him! He looks like an older version of your dad." Which was an even older version of Lorcan; the three men all favored each other so.

"I guess everyone decided to come out anyway...but where will they put everything, and how can we possibly have a party amongst all that charred wood?" Lorcan asked. "Everyone has bags filled with the scavenger hunt prizes as well."

Suddenly an old Rolls Royce came slowly down the street, and as it came closer, I noticed Adriana inside with my great-grandfather Antonio by her side. Keisha Holcomb was driving and had a wide grin on her face, her eyes dancing with excitement.

By the time Lorcan and I reached the burned-out gazebo, everyone who had received the notes and participated in the scavenger hunt and a few that hadn't gathered on the village square; faces joyful. The air was redolent with anticipation. My great-grandparents' car came to a stop just in front of the gazebo. Keisha hurried to open the door and help Antonio from the back seat, handing him his cane and settling him onto a bench while Adriana got out of her own accord.

"Well. It is nice to see everyone having a spark of whimsy and a bit of adventurous spirit, is it not?" Adriana stated as she walked over to me.

"But why? Why bother coming out at all? It's not like we've figured out who was behind all this, and I doubt we will be having a party with the town ravaged as if the Blitz came." I cried. Adriana just winked at me and had a knowing look in her eyes that made me wonder if she'd found something out in the interim since our last meeting.

"Liliana. Vieni qua. Come here." Antonio called over to me, and I rushed to be at his side. "Come. You sit. You read...no?" He handed me a note that was suspiciously like the ones that had shown up all over town as I gawked at him but acquiesced. "You read."

I read it once in my head, then in a loud voice, read the note for everyone gathered to hear:

AT LAST, TOGETHER, SIDE BY SIDE WITH GLEE
FAMILY, FRIENDS...YET STILL...MYSTERY
PIECES OF PUZZLES AND TRINKETS FOR THE PRIZE
BUT NO ONE HAS GONE...AND SOUGHT OUT
THE WISE
(If you know where to look, despite the riddles in that book,
the last piece to bring this all together is right here in plain
sight. Look for the wise one to start this merry night!)

"BUT WHAT DOES IT MEAN?" Asked Andrea. "Who is the wise one?"

We all started gazing around as Keisha and my great-grandfather nodded in encouragement.

"You are behind this! Both of you!" I cried in relief, knowing it wasn't some malevolent dark entity coming for my loved ones. "But why?"

"Your great-grandad was pretty upset with talk of your going off with your aunt and cousins on a ski trip. Adriana was glum about both families squabbling over who was going to get you for Christmas, and she knew you had made so many friends since you've been here that you might not want to be with your family, but with them instead, so she was grumpy. So grumpy, it affected her beloved Antonio and spurred him into action." Keisha stated, laughter bubbling up and out of her. "The two of us realized we had dark humor

118

and practical jokes in common, so we set this enigmatic campaign in motion, then sat back and watched it take flight.

"Let me tell you! Me slinking around this town and tacking up those notes everywhere? 'Borrowing' keys and having to sneak them back where they belonged? Not to mention making a list of all your family and friends Antonio wanted to make sure attended? I about went nuts with all this espionage. Thankfully Joe, here, helped me out, along with Ms. Alessi."

Joe! Tanaquil! I knew he was too relaxed about his waitress and the rest of the town freaking out over the scavenger hunt. He was in on it all along. And Tanaquil. She told me one of my family members was behind it all and not to fuss!

"But...so what do we do now? We have a ruined square. I don't think anyone can fix this. Wise or not! Who could manage it? Who?" Who!

Owls go who or hoot as it were. Owls! *They* were wise. Wait a minute!

"The owl! Did you put it back yet?"

I saw the appreciative gaze my great grandfather lobbed at me, yet at the same time, he shrugged as if to say, 'I don't know...you go see.'

Everyone began to talk at once, and my friends and family began rushing over to the pillar under the clock tower where the small creche opening was. It no longer stood empty but indeed had the newly polished owl back in its rightful place. Upon closer inspection, I realized something was lying across his open claws and reached up to bring it down, holding it carefully in my grip. It was a wand.

Everyone was oohing and ahhing as I walked back over to my favorite gnome and handed the rod over to him. Beaming up at me, Antonio clasped the wand and waved it around above his head in a circle. Nothing happened at first, but suddenly all the tiny trinkets that people had gathered rose out of bags and boxes and danced across the sky to land on the bruised and battered and somewhat scorched fir tree that had decorations on it before the havoc firestorm rendered it useless.

The minute the ornaments alighted onto the branches, something glorious happened. The tree came back to life! Twinkle lights wrapped around the branches and began to glow. At the same time, all traces of scorched wood disintegrated, leaving pine needles a rich green, the tiny ornaments transformed into magnificent decorations. The gazebo revived with a pristine paint job, and everything that had gotten damaged suddenly seemed whole again.

Tables appeared out of nowhere, draped in gold material adorned with silver snowflakes, and friends and family rushed over to place their casseroles and dishes filled with delightful treats on top. Place settings showed up next, and then candelabras with tapers all aglow. Christmas music began to play, and on either side of the sitting area, giant fireplaces manifested complete with crackling logs, snapping, and fizzing, the smoke curling up and out of tall chimneys. Wicked appeared out of nowhere and curled up near one fire. I swear she had a smile on her face.

Glancing around the town, I realized, along with everyone else, that Antonio fully restored it slightly better than it had been before. Take that Witch Council. I doubted if they'd get on Antonio's back for this utterly magical performance. No pun intended.

It was magical. It was breathtaking. And then, to top it all off, it began to snow. Big, beautiful snowflakes commenced falling from the sky and covered the ground in a blanket of white faster than any snow ever had the right to do. Yet, nothing impeded our festivities and merrymaking. The roads remained clear. And the air? It warmed to levels that didn't have any of us shivering despite the spectacle around us.

The feast was extravagant as more and more people arrived, yet there seemed to be plenty of seating and a place-setting for all. Food and drink were bountiful, and everyone was in high spirits. I lost count of the faces, and names didn't matter after a while.

I did note that everyone I knew and loved had indeed shown up, and even those I thought should have received an invite like Rita and Samantha were present. Rowdy Harpin was dancing with his wife, and cousin Sophia was dancing in a circle. She was on her fourth glass of wine. Her husband Sebastiano was clapping at her performance. He'd drunk quite a bit of the grape as well. Andrea ran over to me and pointed out even old Doc Warren, the retired pharmacist, and his sour wife was present. Antonio was graciously regaling them with tales of his plans for a new bocce court, Adriana by his side—having long-forgiven him for being left out of his scheme.

Brian was here in an official capacity, yet he caught my eye, giving me a little salute.

Martha brought a date and had yet to introduce me to her mystery man. Speaking of dates, good old Stu showed up with his secret girlfriend that only I was aware of, shocking his sisters, Sheila and Shirley, speechless. Gordy just smiled knowingly, so I suspected he'd known all along.

Jake and Becky kept making moony eyes at each other, and I wondered when they were going to get around to dating. I didn't think we'd have much longer to wait.

Cousin Flora was making eyes at Steve Junior—a tad creepy considering their age difference and how we were related. Although not by blood, it was still awkward. I was happy to see our resident Lothario had no intention of acknowledging her advances!

There were so many other relatives here that I'd forgotten I'd met and certainly could not put a face to a name, so I gave up and just assumed if I didn't know them already, we were indeed kin. Speaking of kin, I was shocked to see the two captivating sisters, Hortense, and Hermione had decided to convince Old Frank to show up—with his dog pack. None of the partygoers minded the canine companions, well, except for Wicked. She sat spitting at any of them when they came close to where she continued to remain perched on one of the massive fireplace hearths.

Doreen and Donald had imbued quite a bit of the spiked eggnog and began singing Christmas carols, and Susanne Washington joined in with her nephew, Doc Holcomb, following suit. Pretty soon, the entire crowd had voices raised, carols going strong, and I found myself near the gazebo. I decided to join Lorcan, who had climbed the steps.

"This is amazing. Just amazing. I am so thrilled to be part of this wacky family and have all these wonderful friends." I told him as he pulled me into a brief hug. "When I think of what last Christmas was like, I just, I..."

I choked a bit with unshed tears, but Lorcan pulled me in for another hug and hushed them, giving me comfort with his incredible empath abilities.

"Hush, Lily. That is all in your past. This is your future now. Here, in Sweet Briar with your family and friends. Even if we are all insane." He smiled, and my gaze went up to his eyes then continued up as I noticed a bit of green and red dangling above the two of us. Mistletoe!

My eyes widened, and Lorcan glanced up as well.

I don't know if it was the wine that had been flowing or the events of the last few weeks coming to a head, but Lorcan's eyes grew serious as he whispered a soft, "Merry Christmas, Lily." Then he leaned down and kissed me gently on the lips. It was sweet and tender, and I didn't want it to end. We both pulled back, wonder reflecting in both of our eyes, but the moment was lost when a loud explosion rocked the night sky.

"Fireworks!" I cried. "Oh, Lorcan, look!" I pointed up but need not bother, as the spectacle brought on by my diminutive great-grandfather lit the sky around us with a light show to end all light shows. Stu was ecstatic and dancing around with his eggnog, making whooping noises at the sky.

"Merry Christmas, Lorcan! Merry Christmas, indeed!"

We stood a moment longer, just gazing at each other, and I knew this turn of events was something I definitely would have to think long and hard on. For now, I smiled, watching as Lorcan ran down the steps to embrace his parents and grandfather and join in the merrymaking. I looked up at the sky once more and appreciated the jubilation Stu felt at this pyrotechnic display. It was stellar.

As my gaze came back down to earth, I noticed a figure dressed in a white coat huddled in the doorway of my hostile relations beautician shop. Nora! I couldn't see her face, but I could feel her longing. Yet, at the same time, I could sense the negative energy swirling around her. I felt it radiating off of her in waves of hate that headed in my direction. I knew she must have seen me with Lorcan, and I wondered at what mischief she'd get up to when we next would meet. I hoped nothing too devastating. I blinked, and when I scanned the area where she had been standing moments before, I found it empty. Nora had gone.

I'd worry about this development another time. Right now, I was too distracted with the celebration and let myself relax, enjoying the night. I knew I would have to confront my wayward cousin sooner or later, but I deserved this respite and bit of pleasure right now. Too often, my life had been strife and worry. I wouldn't let it cloud this moment.

The partying went on for some time, but then Adriana

rose and, clearing her throat, garnered everyone's attention. "If you please...everyone, quiet a moment." She began.

"I want to thank you on behalf of my beloved Antonio. Indeed he, with Keisha Holcomb, came up with the notes and puzzles and taught us all a lesson, it seems, because the only prize we received is time to gather and cherish friendship and family. My family is blessed, and with the return of our Liliana, I hope this upcoming year brings us all health, wealth, and happiness. I am very grateful to you all and wish every one of you a very Merry Christmas!" She finished, raising her glass high in the air.

"Hear, hear!"

"Cheers!"

"Salute!"

A resounding wave of good cheer filled the square, and everyone drank a toast to good health, love, and peace.

Since the eleventh hour was approaching, the announcement came that Santa would be on his way soon, and, alas, the revelry must come to an end. Sleepy children were bundled up and carried off by parents who still had gifts to place under the tree. Some people went off to midnight services, and others went home to put on Christmas movies. Everyone was sated and happy, and I knew the upcoming year would be one filled with magic in abundance, more magic than I could ever dream possible. And for the first time since I arrived in Sweet Briar, Georgia, I didn't mind one bit.

My name is Lily Sweet, and I'm a witch. And I love it.

Hey! Where did that sheep come from?

* * *

THANK YOU FOR READING! I hope you loved meeting Lily, Adriana, and the rest of the characters. The next book in the

Lily Sweet Mysteries is Sweet Home Liliana. Find out if that kiss will lead to something more! Are Lily and Lorcan destined to be together? Or will Brian Chase come back into play? Lily finally seems to accept who she is...will it last? Or is something coming up that will alter her new outlook?

CLICK HERE TO READ HOW TO SWEET HOME LILIANA, NOW>

And if you enjoyed How to Train Your Witch, you'll love Maggie and her quirky, sometimes funny, sometimes dark, but always magical paranormal gang of monster-hunting antique appraisers. A Tale of Two Sisters, the tie-in series to my Lily Sweet World, highlights Lily's cousins Maggie and Ellie Fortune and is FREE on Kindle Unlimited!

"I AM LOVING the snark in this book."
- S. Keller, BookBub author reviews.

I APPRECIATE your help in spreading the word, including telling friends and family. Reviews help readers find books! Please leave a review on your favorite book site.

YOU CAN ALSO JOIN my Facebook Group: Author Bettina M. Johnson's Team Wicked for exclusive giveaways and sneak peek of future books—and just plain silliness!

SIGN UP FOR BETTINA M. JOHNSON'S NEWS-LETTER: http://eepurl.com/gZKo51

CONTINUE on for a short excerpt from Sweet Home Liliana...

Sweet Home Liliana

I FELT myself pitching forward into the turquoise depths of the pond and knew I would be in trouble if the lady that lived at the bottom refused to come to my aid. My lungs were already aching, and I felt myself panic. Thrashing about in an attempt to make it back to the surface, I wondered if anyone would think to look for me here when I turned up missing—if they looked for me at all.

I knew I didn't have long for this world, so I reached up, desperately trying to grab onto a branch above me, only to have my hand wrap around a dagger which cut deeply into my flesh. Where did that come from? Suddenly, the siren was before me, and I felt the briefest moment of hope. Surely, she would breathe for me as she'd done once before! I reached my arms out toward her, but instead of aid, the pale creature bared razor-sharp teeth and attacked, driving me down to the bottom of the mere. The force of descent pushing at me until my chest felt like it would cave in.

I... wait a minute. I could hear birdsong and a chainsaw in the distance. A car radio carried the dulcet voice of some unknown country singer up to my ears. I'm not in a pond. I'm in bed. I must have been dreaming but "Ow!" What the...?

"Get off me, you stupid cat! What is wrong with you? I'm bleeding!" For some reason, only Wicked, my sleek, black feline comprehends, she had awakened me yet again with claws, teeth, and... "Drool? Did you drool on me? Like the biting and scratching aren't enough, you have to slobber all over me like a dog?" That assertion did me no favors as Wicked took one last swipe at my chin, hopped down off my bed, and ran to the bedroom door where she sat.

"Seriously? You did this to me just to have me let you out? I'm going to bring you to Doc Holcomb and have him rabies test you, you vicious...oof!" Wicked flew back on the bed, where she proceeded to spring onto my head, spun around like a whirling dervish, then launched off my chest like a bolt of lightning, only to sit by the door once more. This time she acted like she didn't have a care in the world and began to wash.

"That's my blood that you're cleaning off your fur, you nasty, despicable beast!"

I've been similarly awakened for the last week now, ever since I packed my meager belongings, Wicked included, and moved into my family home, saying goodbye to my apartment at June's Emporium. I've lived there since returning to Sweet Briar, Georgia, my hometown. June Carter and her husband Dennis live next door above his hardware store, and I'd stayed in the apartment over June's business. A hodge-podge of everything you'd ever hope to find in a small-town general store, and then some.

The Carter's son, Jake, attorney extraordinaire and one of the first persons I'd met when arriving in Georgia, suggested the apartment while I figured out my future. June was my mother's best friend when they were young women growing up. I couldn't ever recall living in this town until about four and a half months ago, when my memories returned after being erased by a meddling witch. They came in small fits, but I remember being in this home when I was a little girl.

I am ensconced in what used to be my Aunt Adelaide's bedroom. The nursery is tiny, and the master bedroom is too reminiscent of my parents living there to feel comfortable making it my own. Adelaide's old room was slightly larger than the master anyway, had beautiful dormers and a better view of the back yard, so I might just keep it. All the rooms had private bathrooms, so either of the larger of the two would work. I was about to start renovations and began each day filled with happy anticipation.

However, that joy was becoming tempered as I started to

wonder if I would ever awaken in the usual manner ever again. Bunking with my furious feline had been tortuous. Leaving her out of my bedroom hadn't worked, either. She just protested until I let her back in again.

Every day Wicked repeated her agitated morning ritual until I'd open the door. Then she would proceed to harangue me by meowing loudly and pawing at an old chest of drawers on the landing. That the drawer held items my mother left for me along with the things I'd found in this home, items I was trying to ignore, was not lost on me. I'd already concluded that Wicked was no ordinary cat. She was magical. Her ability to comprehend was uncanny. But considering I am now comfortable with my witchy world, I couldn't deny having a magical cat was something that would cause me a shock.

Nothing surprised me anymore.

Yes. Magic and witches. I know, right? I, Lily Sweet, am a witch. A dark one. I am not evil, myself. But I am just wicked enough to battle dark forces if and when they decide to enter my little world. And now, I can. I'm finally adept at elemental spells and learning more every day. I come from a long line of witches and have decided I no longer need to check into a mental institution and have my head examined. I've embraced my heritage and all things witch. Even though I didn't grow up a witch, I have accepted the arcane and outré in my world—not to mention family and go with the flow. Honestly? I'm starting to enjoy it.

I am not enjoying being secretive, however. My reticence in sharing the items I've hidden away has more to do with what transpired when I handled them. Plus, I neglected to mention any of this to my great-grandmother, Adriana Dolce —the matriarch of the Dolce clan. I hadn't told anyone in my family. Now? How do I even mention these odd occurrences and the bloody dagger part and parcel among these objects?

After looking through the contents that included the dagger and finding a makeshift map that led me to Nichols Pond, I found a small box that held a ring hidden in the silt. This adventure sounds innocuous until you realize just how deep the water is and that a siren helped me to the bottom to retrieve it. The box the ring came in had a sharp protrusion, and when I accidentally pricked my finger on it, reality shifted, transporting me to an altered state. Cue the fairy tale moment! A voice, which could only be that of my Aunt Adelaide, began to speak, reminding me that I still had to find and release her and find my dad using the ring for guidance.

Find them alive or dead was the question of the hour.

My Aunt Adelaide and father might both be dead, but they also might be alive somewhere with memories erased. Although, if the voice I heard was Aunt Addy, how could this be? Surely the otherworldly voice meant she was no longer in the present. Unless magic was afoot, that is. Adelaide was a dark witch as well, so anything is possible.

I know! I'm horrible! I am not procrastinating or purposely being obtuse out of laziness. I just didn't know how to bring up a subject that will undoubtedly upset my relatives. The horror of what had happened to my father and aunt has shocked and saddened everyone I loved, making the guilt of what I've concealed unbearable. The loss of my mom to cancer was still fresh on their minds, too, after all. I felt like the bearer of bad news and unremitting drama since coming to Sweet Briar. So, I thought it best if I eased them into this latest bit of information.

Although I could just hear myself trying to explain this to my family, "by the way, I know I should have told you sooner, but after I got caught up in a few murders and almost died, I had to deal with a monumental amount of lessons and a Christmas scavenger hunt. And did you know I found a bloody dagger, am hearing voices, have a murderous cat, met a siren, and I now own another magical ring?"

I suppose my relatives might take this in stride. Still, I'm afraid they'd hunt down the mermaid and bring her harm. Especially since they usually eradicate rogue dark sirens to prevent them from using their powerful voices to influence unsuspecting victims. I didn't want that on my head, especially as she had saved my life! But what worried me the most was having my friends and family think to themselves, "Did she not just finish with one mysterious drama, only to have another pop up to trouble us again?" A small part of me worried they might believe I made it up, seeking even more attention.

No really.

It had been one thing after another as of late. I seem to be a magnet for negative energy in the form of evil asshats who kept trying to do me in. I wanted to give the family a break from yet another crisis. But things just kept occurring, and I'm starting to get a complex.

The only three people who knew about all the items, other than my great granny, who was still irritated that I hadn't mentioned them sooner, were Jake, my cousin Andrea, and my friend and landlord, Lorcan Reid. Lorcan had graciously let me rent a warehouse connected to his mechanic shop that used to belong to his grandfather Malcolm. He let me rent at a ridiculously low price, allowing me to get it up and running, although I seemed to make most of my meager sales online or during our many festivals. Our town was known for throwing several every year, and business was booming for many shop owners.

I was happily ensconced in my craft and enjoyed the lull in tourism since it was still winter. With the slow-down in foot traffic, my focus became home renovation and repair. I had to do something with my parents' home, now mine. If I ignored the leaks and suspected termite infestation any longer, I might not have a place to call home! I didn't want anything to distract my mission, and I refused to entertain the idea of ominous trinkets left for me to discover by my mother or her accomplice. I still hadn't figured out who could have been helping my mother all these years, and it wasn't like they were forthcoming, so my life continued to be ruled by mystery and intrigue.

That's why I tucked the items deep in the bottom drawer and tried to forget all about them. Unfortunately, I live in a house with someone who will not let me forget.

Wicked is forcing me to call a family meeting and play Show-and-Tell. It has become her objective. When I am not looking, she has tried tripping me, startling me, or outright attacking me any time I go anywhere near the landing. Her contempt is palpable. Her terror campaign is ruthless and unwavering. Unless she gets hungry, that's when she flips her switch and is all lovey until she finishes partaking a meal. Then it's on again in earnest.

Is it any wonder that nightly I suffer from nightmares repeating all that had transpired?

How that cat is aware of what I'm hiding and why she is determined to have me address them is a mystery! Why couldn't I have a friendly feline companion whose worst transgression was getting into my yarn and ruining my knitting project? Not that I have any yarn or know how to knit. But come on! I already have way too much paranormal in my world to be dealing with an intelligent cat with a penchant for stirring up things that are best left unstirred.

To compound matters, the day I unpacked those objects, holding them in my hand, I could swear I saw what a ghost manifest in the upper hallway.

Yeah. I know! Freaky!

Screaming, I dropped the box and ran downstairs like I

was trying to avoid Peppy le Pew. What? It was frightening. Anyone would have done the same faced with my situation.

One minute there was nothing in the hall, and the next instant, a wispy puff of smoke turned into the figure of a female and popped up out of my heart of pine floor that I had just waxed. She drifted toward me, and I knocked my coffee cup over, then watched it pool all over my newly cleaned floor. My pissed-off disposition at this lasted all of one second because, yeah...ghost coming at me.

Uh, heck yeah, I ran!

Obviously, my cat wants me to go insane by forcing this on me. By making me touch the items, calling the ghost chick so it could moan and groan, I would have no choice but to try and speak with it. The ghost of Edith Plank, the recently murdered town librarian, haunted me for a time, but I couldn't hear a thing she was trying to say to me, not for her lack of trying. Nothing Edith said crossed whatever veil separated us—she on one side, and me firmly, and thankfully, on the other. I managed to help her find some peace by solving her murder. Well, sort of. And she had since departed for the great beyond. There was no way I would tackle another ghost on my own. It wasn't going to happen.

You see, there was only one female murdered and buried on this property that I know of anyway. Let's face it, with my family's reputation, who knew? So that meant, if I was correct in my deduction, I was dealing with the ghost of Deanna Fredricks. Insane Donna's little sister. Deanna was the person responsible for charming my Aunt Adelaide and father Charlie, erasing their memories and sending them off to their doom. Or at the very least, to a new life where they had no recollection of who they were or from where they came. Donna tried to kill me when I first moved to town, and she was the one who not only murdered her sister but hid her remains under my side porch. Hence, Deanna's ghost.

I did not want to deal with this creature. Because if it were a repeat of the Edith fiasco, I wouldn't be able to hear her speaking to me, and I didn't relish the thought of playing charades with the ghost of the person tantamount to the destruction of my family.

Squaring my shoulders, I had just prepared myself to ignore Wicked's list of kitty grievances and march downstairs to make coffee when I heard a loud knock on the back door. None of my friends or family ever used the front door since my occupying the house, choosing the entry which took them through the mudroom and into my welcoming kitchen. So I assumed it must be one or the other.

I steadfastly ignored glancing at the drawers as I passed and lightly ran down the front steps, flying through the living and dining rooms, and skidded into the kitchen, where I came to an abrupt halt. Confronted with the number one reason I had indigestion regularly was standing at the spot where a stove should be. My great-grandmother, Adriana, stood there in all her glory. It seems her waiting for me to invite her inside hadn't crossed her mind, and she decided to enter my home. That this used to be her house wasn't lost on me; a place she inherited from her parents and kept in the family even after marrying my great-grand-father, Antonio, and moved to the family Victorian across town.

This home was a craftsman mission style built around 1908 when my great-grandmother was a little girl. Yes. I know what that dates might imply. No, I'm not about to ask her exact age. Witches lived very long lives, and as she has informed me more than once, she is just hitting her prime. Who am I to argue the point? Adriana could probably take me in an arm-wrestling competition, and she runs around town like a little petite dynamo.

"Good morning, granny. To what do I owe the pleasure?"

"You have no appliances. When are you going to get around to ordering some?"

Or not.

"I've only been here a week. I'm not sure what my plans are for this big renovation project yet, so I thought it was prudent to..."

"And the windows. You have no draperies or adornment of any kind. It's so drafty. I went to put the coffee on, but I can't find the espresso maker."

Someone was just as cranky as me when suffering from a java deficiency, so I thought to cut her some slack.

"I have a single brew coffee station over here and can..."

"Where are your cups? Spoons? Don't you have any utensils? How are you living without proper utensils?"

"Grandmother. Is there any reason you are here so early in the morning critiquing my lack of proper kitchen implements? What's wrong?"

Because even for you, this seems a bit much, lady. And plastic spoons and forks are utensils—sort of.

"What makes you think there is something wrong?"

"Why are you getting defensive with me asking you a legitimate question by asking one of your own?" I countered.

"I'm not getting defensive, and you just asked one yourself."

"Yes, you are."

"No, I'm not; you're so difficult."

"I'm difficult? You waltz in here at seven in the morning on a Monday and start assessing everything, and I'm difficult?"

"I'm making friendly observations. I can't help it if you are a whiny baby."

"I'm not whining."

"Yes, you are...whiner."

Wait. Enough. Someone had to be the mature one around

here, or this could go on into next year, and as we were still in January, it would be a long, drawn-out battle.

"Alright. Stop. Grandmother, just sit over here in the den, and I will bring us some coffee so we can talk. Please? Something has you troubled. Just go settle yourself in one of those cozy chairs, and I will be right with you."

I rushed around the kitchen preparing coffee—yes, I owned mugs, two as a matter of fact—and grabbed some store-bought biscotti, which I hoped would soothe Adriana's prickly demeanor. Once I had the fixings prepared, I brought everything into the den and sat opposite my great-grandmother so we could talk about what was vexing her. I set my mug, one that had a chip I hoped she wouldn't notice, near my spot, then placed her cup in front of where she was seated and watched as she sniffed my offering with suspicion before taking a sip. She smiled, giving me begrudged approval. She turned up her nose at the store-bought cookies, however, but I could only do so much.

"Now. Talk. What's up?"

Granny took another delicate sip of coffee before sitting back and scrutinizing me for a long minute. Then she proceeded to tell me about her morning.

"I have just left your Aunt Chiara. She was telling me you've all but refused to take the mantle and run the DFD Foundation & Trust. I didn't have the heart to tell her I'm with you on that one. You seem to be a tad too young to be stuck in a board room listening to old witches blather on about their sciatica or incontinence. She's been doing a great job controlling the daily minutiae. I think she's secretly relieved you didn't want to step in and take charge. You will have to someday, but for now, she'll do."

And?

I waited for Adriana to go on, but she settled deep into the cushions of her chair and drank her coffee. This behavior, this reticence, especially for my straightforward and crafty great-grandmother, was unusual. So, I knew whatever she was putting off telling me had to be significant. As much as I wanted to move the conversation along, I wisely held my tongue and was rewarded for my patience when prolonged silence was enough to induce Adriana to continue. My satisfaction dampened when she revealed why she was out of sorts.

"Before I left, the phone rang. Chiara answered as I was walking past her, and she grabbed onto my sleeve, stopping me in my tracks. It was the Witch Council. They have news of your father and Aunt Adelaide. And it's not good."

* * *

SOCIAL MEDIA LINKS

I write in my own style that may not be everyone's cup of tea —so if you enjoy my characters and humor, my plots, how the storyline is developing, etc. and are eagerly anticipating the next in the series, be aware that I am just as excited as you are—I've found someone who thinks my story ideas are neat! That is thrilling for any writer to know (or it should be). THANK YOU!

Visit my official website to receive updates, find out about special offers and new releases, or read my blog about writing and farm life - complete with photos - you might even catch me mowing my ten acres (seriously): http://www.bettinamjohnson.net

For more information or to contact me:
author@bettinamjohnson.net

For even more (if you just can't enough of me) follow my
Social Media Links

Mailing List - https://bit.ly/2BvQXmP
BookBub - https://bit.ly/2Epejwj
Goodreads - https://bit.ly/3aTejQW
Author Page - Amazon - https://amzn.to/3lj7L2L
Instagram - https://bit.ly/2QpZa01
TikTok - https://bit.ly/2PQa6Hg
MeWe - https://bit.ly/36A2RcM
Facebook - https://bit.ly/3gOaFZY
Twitter: https://bit.ly/3jahMgY
YouTube - https://bit.ly/2Stvy2X

ABOUT THE AUTHOR

I always knew I wanted to write. As a kid, way before the technology age had hit, I'd be stuck in the car with the folks as we drove from our home on Staten Island, NY, where I was born and raised, to our family property in the Catskill Mountains. To drive away boredom, I would sit, staring out the window, and create adventures of daring thieves riding horseback along the road, trying to escape the law. Other times I'd imagine a wild girl riding her unicorn into battle (I had a vivid imagination - we didn't have video games yet!).

As the years passed, I'd start writing a book, then stop, then start again only to let life get in the way, until one day I had an epiphany—a kick in the pants moment. If I waited any longer, all those wonderful characters in my head would never have their stories told, and that made me sad. So, I treated writing as my career. Once I started, it became apparent nothing would ever stop me again. YOU, dear reader, are stuck with me until I go off to that great library in the sky...or wherever writers go when they crumble to dust in front of their typewriters (or laptops...whatever!).

I live in the North Georgia mountains on what I like to call a farm, with my husband and almost adult kids, a Cairn Terrier, a bunch of cats, and fish. Occasionally other critters show up to keep things exciting.

BOOKS BY BETTINA M. JOHNSON

The Lily Sweet Mysteries:

Home Sweet Witch

Witch Way is Up?

How To Train Your Witch

Sweet Home Liliana

Witch Way Did He Go? (Coming Soon)

* * *

The Fortune-Telling Twins Mysteries:

A Tale of Two Sisters